When Make-Believe Turns Real

"So we're back to square one, are we?" asked Eyre. "Madly in love again."

"If you must put it that way," Darryn said, biting her lip. "But I'm not going to pretend to be engaged to you."

"I'll keep that in mind," he said gravely.

They began to walk on again, and he put his arm around her waist and murmured persuasively, "Wouldn't you like to be engaged to me, Darryn?"

"Definitely not," she said, hoping he didn't notice how sensitive she was to his nearness. "Not even for a—a week or whatever you had in mind."

"Suppose I said forever?"

DOROTHY CORK

was born in Australia and has lived there most of her life. Her many readers may well have guessed this as her entertaining novels are frequently set in her native land. Not that she limits herself to this region. She is an enthusiastic and perceptive traveler. Her wholehearted enjoyment of life is reflected in her lively romances.

Dear Reader:

I'd like to take this opportunity to thank you for all your support and encouragement of Silhouette Romances.

Many of you write in regularly, telling us what you like best about Silhouette, which authors are your favorites. This is a tremendous help to us as we strive to publish the best contemporary romances possible.

All the romances from Silhouette Books are for you, so enjoy this book and the many stories to come. I hope you'll continue to share your thoughts with us, and invite you to write to us at the address below:

Karen Solem
Editor-in-Chief
Silhouette Books
P.O. Box 769
New York, N.Y. 10019

DOROTHY CORK
Outback Dreaming

Silhouette Romance

Published by Silhouette Books New York

America's Publisher of Contemporary Romance

SILHOUETTE BOOKS, a Division of Simon & Schuster, Inc.
1230 Avenue of the Americas, New York, N.Y. 10020

Copyright © 1983 by Dorothy Cork

Distributed by Pocket Books

ISBN: 0-671-57238-5

First Silhouette Books printing August, 1983

10 9 8 7 6 5 4 3 2 1

Map by Ray Lundgren

America's Publisher of Contemporary Romance

Printed in the U.S.A.

Other Silhouette Books by Dorothy Cork

Secret Marriage
By Honour Bound
Reluctant Deceiver
No More Regrets
Island Spell

Outback
Dreaming

TIMOR SEA

CORAL SEA

NORTHERN
TERRITORY

Alice
Springs

QUEENSLAND

INDIAN OCEAN

WESTERN
AUSTRALIA

SOUTH
AUSTRALIA

PACIFIC OCEAN

Brisbane

NEW SOUTH
WALES

Perth

Adelaide

Sydney
Canberra

VICTORIA

Melbourne

TASMAN
SEA

AUSTRALIA

Chapter One

"Don't take any pictures of Eyre Madison, Darryn,"
Margo Talbot said. "Or disaster will surely follow."

Darryn laughed and took it lightly at the time, but
later she was to think that Margo had been right.
Disaster did follow. As it was, she merely paused and
looked at her employer politely.

Margo was middle-aged with blonded hair, a large
bust, and an extrovert personality. Darryn, at twenty,
found her just a little intimidating, but was grateful to
have the opportunity of working for her, thanks to the
fact that she'd long ago been a friend of the woman
Darryn had worked for in Sydney.

"A lady with lots of originality" was how June
Stevens had described her to Darryn. "You should get
on well with her. She's a lot of fun and very innovative.
She'll allow you to stretch your wings and do things
your own way."

It was all true enough, as Darryn had discovered
after only five days in Alice Springs. Not for Margo the
conventional wedding groups, the carefully posed portraits, the recording of angelic children. Margo had her
own ideas and they were individual and often way out.
Yet people flocked to her from all over the Northern

Territory. Darryn was enjoying working with her and hoped fervently she'd be asked to stay on, for she was only on trial to begin with.

Today they were spending a couple of hours at the rodeo, taking pictures for the local paper and for the social pages of a woman's magazine published in Adelaide.

"Straight pictures today," Margo had remarked before they set out from Todd Street in Alice Springs, Margo in her disreputable old Ford, Darryn on the motorcycle she'd hired—and of which she was more than a little afraid—in the hopes that she'd be able to explore in her spare time and perhaps find Moon Mountain cattle station—a secret desire that was very personal and very close to her heart. "Lots of city visitors at this function—they want to be pictured in the right company, wearing the right clothes, and impressing their friends back home. I'll clue you up on a few bigwigs, local and otherwise, and after that you can play it by ear."

Now, at the grounds some miles outside the town where the rodeo in aid of the Royal Flying Doctor Service was being held, she gave Darryn a final briefing.

"Eyre Madison doesn't like having his picture in the local paper, or anywhere else, for that matter. I can't spot him just at the moment, but he'll be somewhere around. He always patronises any function held in aid of the R.F.D.S. You'll have no trouble recognising him anyhow. He has—"

She broke off suddenly as a woman in a huge organza hat that reminded Darryn of a bedroom lampshade clutched her by the arm.

"Margo darling! I've been hunting for you for at least half an hour. The Hayes-Thomases are here from Katherine and we're all dying to have you take some gorgeous piccies. Patty's engaged to Bill at last, and we want it known. I've got the whole family hobbled under the trees with half a dozen bottles of champagne and my best crystal goblets. Crazy, but it *is* an occasion. You simply must come before Tom succumbs—you know what he's like!"

Margo walked off, turning briefly to send Darryn a cheery little wave of her hand; and left alone, Darryn wondered how on earth she was meant to recognise Eyre Madison, whoever he was. Well, it didn't matter all that much. He'd probably let her know soon enough if she was intruding on his privacy.

She began to move across the stiff grass of the paddock towards the railed area where the rodeo events were taking place, and it wasn't long before, identified by her professional-looking camera, she was besieged by very normal people who were eager to have their photographs taken.

When at last she had a breathing space, she went to lean against the rail and relax and take in the rodeo scene. Here in the hot sun of the Red Centre, she had an excited sense of being where she truly belonged. She was going to stay in the Northern Territory forever! It was her part of the world, and she was quite positive that the feeling wouldn't wear off in spite of her mother's skepticism.

"You won't like the outback, Darryn. The glamour will soon disappear and you'll wish you'd never given up your job in Sydney. You'll be just as disillusioned as I was twenty-one years ago when I ran away, thinking I'd had all I wanted of study and city life. It was totally disastrous. But I suppose like all young people you'll have to learn from your own experience."

Darryn had listened without comment. Since she was one of the results of her mother's disastrous visit to the outback, she had a kind of vested interest in it. At any rate, she wasn't running away from anything.

She was fond of her parents. Her mother had mar-

ried Richard Ross when Darryn was five, and he'd
adopted her legally. Both he and her mother were very
different from Darryn. In fact, the only similarity
between herself and her mother was the fact that they
both had bright red-gold hair. Her mother lectured in
economics, and her father in English, but Darryn was
no academic. She appreciated the fact that they'd let
her go her own way and take up photographic work, an
interest that had been stimulated by her grandfather,
with whom she'd spent most of her school holidays.

For her, this journey to the outback was a search for
her real self—the self that was akin to her father. And
though she certainly didn't expect to find *him,* she was
still his daughter and she felt herself attached by fate to
the place where she'd been conceived, a cattle station
called Moon Mountain.

She hadn't dared tell her mother that, and she'd
never confessed to a living soul that Moon Mountain
was the place she thought of secretly as her Dreaming.
It was a strange notion, but it had gradually grown
inside her being and become part of her spiritual
equipment, ever since as a child she'd read of the
Dreaming places that meant so much to the aborigines
—places they believed had been inhabited by their
totemic ancestors away back in the Dreamtime. Sometimes a totemic site was determined for a child by the
mystic fact that he'd been conceived there, and so, in
Darryn's mind, Moon Mountain had become *her*
Dreaming place. It was an irrational belief perhaps, but
it affected her deeply.

Now she gazed about her at the stockmen in curly
brimmed hats and narrow-legged trousers, at the country women in simple cottons and shady hats. My
people, she thought. She felt so much more akin to
them than to the fashion-conscious city-dwellers. What
impression did *she* give? she wondered, thrusting back
the silky strands of red-gold hair that fell across one

delicately tanned cheek. She glanced down at her soft denim-blue dress of fine cotton, her matching blue sandals. Nothing there to catch anyone's eye, she thought wryly, not with her bright hair hidden under the white cotton hat she was wearing.

All the same, a sixth sense told her that *somebody* was looking at her, and she turned her head to see who it was.

Immediately, she felt her nerves leap. It was a man, of course, and as her eyes met his, she had an impression of brilliance and intensity. He was leaning indolently against the rail, some twenty feet away from her, and he continued to stare at her from beneath dark, strongly-marked eyebrows.

Somewhat shaken, Darryn stared back. He didn't move—not so much as an eyelash—and she began to wonder if he saw her at all, or if he was completely lost in his thoughts. Unable to help herself, she studied him in full detail. Hard and lean and casual-looking in tight jeans and dark shirt that emphasised in turn the narrowness of his hips and the muscularity of his shoulders, he had thick smoky brown hair with a startling silver streak over one temple. His face was deeply bronzed, his strikingly good looks given character by a harshness of which she was deeply and instantly aware. Though she was far from being a woman of the world, she somehow knew that he was dynamite, and she just couldn't take her eyes off him. She wished uneasily that he'd move, give some indication that he *saw* her, and wasn't looking through her.

For a long moment, her camera was forgotten. Then, suddenly, she itched to capture him on film, to add his picture to the record she'd been making of her personal life since she was ten years old. She had an uncanny feeling that he was going to make some kind of impact on her life. Who knew what her camera would reveal that she couldn't see with her feminine and prejudiced eye? She was often surprised at the statements her pictures made. Her grandfather, who had been a dedicated amateur photographer, and who had taught her most of what she knew, had discussed this with her more than once; and since his death over a year ago, she had begun slowly to discover what he meant.

"Remember this, Darryn," he had told her. "One should never be surprised at the odd things one wants to capture on film. There's something waiting there in the mind, triggered off by the senses. But so few of us have the ability, or take the time, to heed the messages from our intricate and sensitive thoughts. You'll find what you have the urge to photograph will teach you many things about yourself—your prejudices, your desires, your beliefs."

Darryn was only on the edge of discovering the truth of that, and she wondered now what hidden side of herself might emerge from a photograph of this virile and harshly attractive man. She was piqued, of course, by the fact that though he stared, he didn't appear to be aware of her. If she focussed her camera on him, he just might spring to life.

Instead, he looked away from her and she was forgotten—if he'd noticed her at all. A woman had drifted up to stand gracefully at his side. She had a lovely face, and she wore a droopy brimmed hat that shaded her eyes prettily.

As the man turned to speak to her, she glanced in Darryn's direction, and smiled quickly and gaily, almost as though Darryn were a friend. Darryn smiled back, then suddenly woke up to herself. *That* was a request for a photograph of course! The man's whole attention was on the pretty woman who had laid her hand on his arm and was smiling into his eyes. It was a beautiful pose. They knew each other well, Darryn decided, and they looked perfect together. It would be a lovely shot . . .

At the exact moment she clicked the shutter, the man raised his head and looked in her direction, his expression so enraged that her eyes widened and for a moment she felt completely paralysed. The woman, she noticed, appeared totally unconcerned.

Darryn didn't quite know what to do, and when she recovered the use of her limbs she did the first thing that came into her head. She walked rapidly away. If anything needed to be said, then that man could chase after her. She couldn't be expected to know what was going on, if he was having an affair or something and didn't want it known. This was a public place and she was just doing her job. At all events, Margo was sure to know who these people were, and it would be up to her to decide if they were of any interest to the readers of *Woman and Leisure*. If not, the picture would be scrapped, and that would be that.

She turned her attention determinedly to what was happening in the ring, but she couldn't get that furious look she'd been given out of her mind, and her legs were still slightly unsteady. If looks could kill, she thought, trying to make a joke of it, then she'd be lying in the dust, stone dead. Anyhow, she was going to put the whole thing out of her mind. That man hadn't chased her up, so maybe his companion had pacified him.

She shuddered slightly. He was certainly handsome, but he could also be very unpleasant, that was plain. Which just proved that looks weren't everything.

And now she was going to forget the whole incident. That picture would probably show nothing more than two people smiling at each other pleasantly, anyhow.

Some minutes later, she was more or less caught up in what was taking place beyond the rails, where a young man in a checked shirt, dusty boots and tight pants was throwing a steer. He was on foot, and she watched tensely as he grabbed the weighty, solid-looking animal around the neck and wrestled with it. Man and beast twisted, battled, the dust rose, someone shouted words of encouragement, there was laughter, then a cheer as, at last, when Darryn's nerves had reached screaming point, the beast gave way and fell to the ground.

Darryn heard her own sharp intake of breath as she turned away momentarily. She was thinking of her father—Chris Beresford—whom her mother had met at a rodeo right here in Alice Springs, twenty-one years ago. Had he been engaged in this kind of competition? And had *she* been carried away by his wild and reckless daring? Darryn had no real idea. Her mother never talked about it except in the vaguest of terms, as if the whole business were something she didn't want to be reminded of. Some immature and somehow shameful escapade.

I'll bet he was like that, Darryn thought. *And that he looked at her and she lost her heart.*

Almost unwillingly, she watched the man in the checked shirt wipe the sweat first from his neck and then from his brow, using a dark red handkerchief he pulled out of his pants pocket. She was fascinated, drawn right out of herself into another world—the world where her father had belonged. He'd lived in the outback, taken part in the wild, uncivilised events that made up a country rodeo. And even while one part of her couldn't accept it, deep down inside she exulted in the knowledge that men could be so senselessly courageous. Something in her responded to such recklessness.

She raised her camera, and as the man stood over the fallen beast, she took a picture. Not for Margo Talbot or for any woman's magazine, but for herself. For Darryn Ross who was really Darryn Beresford, daughter of an outback stockman.

She started when a voice behind her made her turn swiftly.

"That shot you took just now—"

Her green eyes flew wide open and her heart began to pound. It was the man with the silver streak in his hair, and he was looking at her intently, his brilliant metallic-blue eyes not quite so furious as they had been, but still far from friendly. Everything she'd been thinking of went out of her head as he stared at her.

Her chin lifted and she felt a thrill of defiance run through her. "The man and the steer? What about it?" she asked, deliberately misunderstanding.

His eyes hardened. "You know what I'm talking about. Nobody gave you permission to take that photograph of me and Mrs. Dwyer. It's not to be used in any way. Is that clear?"

"No, it's not." Darryn felt herself bristle at his tone, and her fingers tightened unconsciously on her camera. From the look on his face, she wouldn't have put it past him to reach out and smash it. It had happened to other people, but never, so far, to her. She didn't believe in invading people's privacy, and she couldn't see that she'd done so now.

Her tongue touched the corner of her mouth. "Mrs. Dwyer wanted the picture. I know because she smiled at me. That's all the *permission* I needed, as far as I'm concerned."

"The lady did not want a photograph," he said distinctly, and Darryn felt antagonism rise in her afresh at his tone.

"I'm afraid you're wrong. She did. So don't try to push me around, just because you're a man and I'm a girl."

His eyes flashed angrily. "A girl? You're an aggressive little reporter. . . . What paper are you representing? If any," he added deliberately.

"Are you putting me down because I'm young now?" she demanded, making no attempt to hide her hostility. "I'm representing the Talbot Studios in Alice Springs. If you want to check, then do so. My name's Darryn Ross. I don't know what foul use you imagine your picture may be put to, but the worst that can happen is for it to appear in *Woman and Leisure*. If it's of any interest to them," she finished, fully aware that she was being impertinent, but thinking it served him right.

He smiled slightly though there were still splinters of ice in his blue eyes. Darryn forced herself to look away from them, and found herself staring instead at his smoky hair with its silver streak. For some reason, she was positive that he must be a wealthy socialite, and that Margo would pounce on his picture with glee.

"So you're working for Margo Talbot," she heard him say dryly. "In that case, there's no more to be said. By me, that is. I can't speak for your employer. And for your information—*if* Mrs. Dwyer smiled at you, it was probably because she thought you were someone she knew. She's shortsighted." With that parting shot, he strode off, leaving her speechless.

She was not sure at what exact point after that she began to suspect he must be Eyre Madison, the man whose precious image was not to be bandied about in women's magazines. It was a fact that no one would have any trouble recognising *him*.

But Darryn Ross hadn't recognised him, and she'd been positively rude to him. Well, she thought defiantly, no harm had been done. Except, presumably, to his ego. No doubt he thought everyone recognised him on sight, and he'd be incredulous if he knew that until today she hadn't even heard of him. Even now, she was ignorant of what claim he had to fame. If any.

At five o'clock, she and Margo met up as prearranged, and Margo suggested she might like to stay on a little longer and enjoy herself.

"Did you meet anyone you particularly liked?" she asked with a meaning smile, and Darryn shook her head. Curiously enough, the man who must be Eyre Madison came into her mind, but she certainly didn't like *him*, and she'd better explain what had happened before Margo discovered her blunder when she was developing the films.

"I think I'd better tell you something," she said, as they began to move towards the trees where the cars were parked. "I think I took a picture of Eyre Madison. That's if he's the man with the silver streak in his hair."

Margo widened her eyes. "Darling—did you do that? That's really naughty. It's just not done to aim your camera at Eyre Madison of Moon Mountain. He doesn't like pictorial speculation about his women friends. Who was he with?" she added, lowering her voice.

For a moment, Darryn was totally incapable of answering. She wasn't even listening. Eyre Madison of Moon Mountain! Had Margo really said that? She didn't want to believe it. Eyre Madison couldn't be connected with Moon Mountain—that mystic romantic place whose name had captured her imagination when she was a child. The place where, she'd realised as she grew older, she'd been conceived. Had Madisons run the cattle station then, she wondered? Her mother had never mentioned any names—probably didn't know any, she'd been there for such a brief time. Barely long enough to get herself pregnant . . .

Margo was staring at her oddly and she realised her face had gone white and that she was biting nervously on her lower lip. She pulled herself together and said hastily, "He was with a Mrs. Dwyer."

"Ellen Dwyer! Oh, I see," Margo exclaimed.

Darryn didn't listen. "You didn't tell me Eyre Madison lived at Moon Mountain," she hurried on. "What does he do there?"

"Why, he runs the place—he owns it," Margo said, looking at her strangely. "What's bothering you, Darryn? If Eyre was annoyed with you, forget it. It wasn't your fault. I seem to remember I didn't quite finish what I was telling you about him. I'll ring around the hotels tonight—he's probably staying at the Federal Casino. I'll apologise, explain. Will that make you feel happier?"

Darryn nodded, but in her imagination she was back at the rails with Eyre Madison, reshaping the conversation she'd had with him. This time, instead of being aggressive and impertinent, as she had been, she was being very pleasant.

"You must be Mr. Madison. I realise that now and I'm most terribly sorry. Mrs. Talbot had begun to tell me about you, but we were interrupted." And then, somehow, she was asking him about Moon Mountain, and he was inviting her on a visit . . .

"Are you coming?" she heard Margo asking her, and she pulled herself together quickly.

"I was just thinking—maybe I will stay on a little longer."

"You might as well," Margo said. "We shan't do anything in the studio tonight. I've been asked out to dinner. We'll make an early start in the morning. Eight o'clock. All right?"

Darryn nodded. "I'll be there."

Margo moved to her car, and Darryn hurried off resolutely in the other direction. She was going to look for Eyre Madison. She'd sink her pride and apologise to him. She had to, if she wanted to get to Moon Mountain. And she wanted it still in spite of him. She'd wanted it for a long long time.

She had no trouble finding him. In fact, she'd taken no more than half a dozen steps when she almost ran into him. Immediately her heart began to beat furiously fast. What on earth was she going to say? It was all very well apologising in her imagination, but when it came to the real thing it was not nearly so easy.

He was looking down into her face, his expression a little amused.

"What's the matter, Miss Ross? Have you got yourself into more trouble with that impertinent tongue of yours?"

"Nothing like that," she retorted, immediately hostile and immediately regretting it. She forced a smile and softened her voice. "I was looking for you, as a matter of fact. I've just been talking to Margo Talbot." She raised her hand nervously to tidy some strands of hair that had escaped from under her hat. "I'd like to apologise for my behaviour a little while ago. I had no idea who you were, you see, and I just thought—well, most people like to have their pictures taken, but now I know you don't. So I wanted to say I'm sorry," she finished, grimacing at her clumsiness and eyeing him from under her long shining lashes.

He rested his hands on his narrow hips and looked back at her impassively.

"You've been given the sack, have you? And you want me to intervene on your behalf—"

Darryn had to bite her lip to prevent herself from answering back. She shook her head and managed to say levelly, "I haven't been sacked. I've only been in Alice Springs a short time, and naturally I didn't know your wishes."

"Very well," he said after a moment. "I'll accept your apology. But I advise you to curb that temper of yours if you want to get on in your profession. It is your profession, I take it. Or are you merely earning a few pennies while you have a holiday?"

"It's my profession," Darryn said. She racked her brains desperately to think of some way to suggest he might invite her to visit Moon Mountain, but she could think of absolutely nothing. Besides, she had the hopeless feeling that no matter what she said, Eyre Madison wouldn't invite her anywhere. He didn't like her any more than she liked him. Probably less. All the same, she had to try, and she suddenly plunged ahead recklessly.

"As a matter of fact, I've been asked by an editor in Sydney to do a feature on outback life. That means I'll have to get out to one or two of the cattle stations, so I'm hoping for an invitation." Even to her own ears, it sounded horribly blatant, but she forced a bright smile and went on determinedly, "I believe you live on a cattle station, Mr. Madison."

"That's right," he agreed. He took cigarettes from his pocket and offered them to her, his narrowed eyes fixed intently on her face as if he were thinking deeply about something. *Ask me,* she prayed inwardly. *Please ask me to Moon Mountain. You must.* She shook her head at the cigarettes, and he put the packet back in his pocket before he said dryly, "Well, I wish you luck, Miss Ross. There are plenty of cattle stations around Alice Springs. I'm quite sure a pretty and determined girl like you will get all the invitations she can handle."

Darryn stared at him. She rarely blushed, but now her face was flooded with colour. Talk about a snub! He knew she'd been fishing for an invitation, and he was making it very plain that she needn't expect one from him. Her apology apparently counted for nothing, and she didn't try to keep the dislike out of her angry green eyes as they met his coolly cynical gaze.

She didn't know what she might have said next if Mrs. Dwyer hadn't appeared then. Darryn suddenly remembered Margo's exclamation—"Ellen Dwyer! Oh, I see!" and she looked at the woman curiously. Where was her husband? Or was she a widow? She ignored Darryn completely, which was hardly polite even if she were shortsighted, Darryn thought. But it was clearly her cue to disappear, and she did so smartly. Without another word to the hateful and unobliging Eyre Madison, she turned on her heel and walked away quickly in the direction of her dreaded motorcycle.

As she skimmed bumpily back along the red dusty road to Alice she felt that everything was suddenly going wrong, and it was all because of that man, Eyre Madison. Why did he have to live at Moon Mountain? And how could she possibly go there now? Her dreams had begun to crumble, nothing was going to be the way she wanted it to be; no door was going to open onto a world where she truly belonged. Her Dreaming had vanished.

So okay, wasn't that life? Wasn't that the sort of thing a mature person should expect? She'd better forget about Moon Mountain and her father and every damned thing. Which was more or less what her mother had been advising her to do for years. "It's all in the past, Darryn. Why let it bother you? You've been cared for, loved. You've had a father, you've been happy."

"But what was my *real* father like?" she'd insisted once. "Why didn't you stay married to him?"

"Our marriage was a mistake," her mother had said. "I was going through a phase where I wanted to shock my parents. Chris and I were both very immature, we'd both left home, but apart from that we knew practically nothing about each other."

There followed a little lecture on the wisdom of getting to know a man before you tied yourself up to him. Nothing about love . . .

And love, Darryn reflected moodily as she drove into Alice Springs, was something she knew very little about. She'd never been in love with anyone. "Darryn's much too interested in her photography to bother about men," she'd heard her mother tell somebody not so long ago. And now, unexpectedly, she thought of Mrs. Dwyer and the way she'd looked at that

man from Moon Mountain, and she was aware of a
strange ache in her heart.

At the motel where she was staying until Margo
decided whether to employ her permanently or not, she
went straight to the shower. She felt exhausted. Her
mind was full of that stupid conversation she'd had with
Eyre Madison, and she wished she were years older and
miles more sophisticated so that she could have—
wound him 'round her little finger, the way beautiful
and sexy women were supposed to be able to do. Who
would he be dining with tonight? she wondered. Mrs.
Dwyer. That was her guess.

But why on earth was she thinking about the man,
she asked herself furiously, as she shampooed her long
red hair. And told herself the answer was because she
was wild that she'd made such a fool of herself.

By the time she'd emerged from the shower, she'd
decided she'd go out somewhere and treat herself to an
expensive meal.

Wrapped in a big blue towel, she opened the wardrobe with one hand and brushed her damp curly hair
with the other. There were lots of things in life besides
going to Moon Mountain, she thought with determined
cheerfulness. She was still glad she'd come to Alice
Springs, and if Margo offered her a job as her permanent assistant she'd take it.

And that idea she'd come up with when she was
talking to Eyre Madison—why shouldn't she follow it
up? She'd already begun to make a minor mark in
circles where black-and-white photography was taken
seriously. She'd exhibited three or four pictures at a
recent show in Sydney and her work had been called
creative. It was true she'd been ad-libbing about the
assignment from a Sydney editor, but the outback
excited her and she was sure she could do some sort of
original and experimental work that would interest
someone . . .

So that man could go jump in the lake. She was disappointed about Moon Mountain of course. More than disappointed. She felt that she'd been robbed of something that she'd treasured in her heart for a very long time.

But sitting here moping wasn't going to mend matters, so Darryn Ross was going out to eat.

She chose a jade green dress that had a deep V-neckline back and front, and slithered into it. Dressing up for no one. Heavens, wasn't she having a fit of the blues tonight! She reached over to switch on the television and the telephone rang.

"Miss Ross? Someone to see you."

"Oh. Who?"

"Mr. Madison."

Darryn nearly collapsed on the bed. Eyre Madison! For a moment she couldn't take it in. What on earth was he doing here? "I—I can't see him for a few minutes," she said wildly. "Tell him to wait in the bar—in the lounge."

"Okay Miss Ross. In the lounge. I'll tell him that."

Darryn stood staring at herself in the big mirror over the long countertop that ran the length of the room and served as dressing table, writing desk and breakfast table. She was tempted to ring back to reception and say she was going out, but she knew she wasn't really likely to do that. Not in a million years. She had to know what he wanted. Maybe he'd changed his mind about ignoring her hints and was going to invite her to Moon Mountain. Maybe he was going to tell her she could use that picture after all, that he and Mrs. Dwyer were going to be married. Maybe anything. Meanwhile she'd better finish dressing.

She took her time over her hair and her make-up. If he chose to call on people unexpectedly then he had to wait. Moreover, she'd tell him she had a dinner date and didn't have a lot of time to spare. Oh yes—she was going to tell him quite a few things, so long as she didn't find herself tongue-tied.

But why on earth should she? She hadn't been tongue-tied this afternoon. Far from it!

Her hair looked great when she'd finished with it. That was, of course, if you liked hair that was so bright it didn't look real. It was the exact colour of her mother's. She'd gone through a period of hating it when she was at school, and when she was thirteen she'd begged to be allowed to dye it. She'd grown up since then, and now she liked her hair. She'd looped it along her cheeks, caught it back in a soft knot low on the back of her head, and fastened it with silvery green leaves that matched her dress.

Her depression had vanished as if by magic and her face was vivid and alive. He probably wouldn't recognise her, she thought with a slight smile. That white hat had made her look really gruesome in an amusing kind of way. Not her style at all.

He came to meet her as she entered the lounge. There were a lot of people around, but most of them were tourists who'd come to Alice to see Standley Chasm and the camel farm and maybe to attend the rodeo. None of them belonged to the social set, because this was an inexpensive motel. Darryn drifted across the carpeted floor, her green eyes starry against the subtle silver eye shadow she'd used, dark mascara emphasising her long lashes. To her annoyance her legs trembled slightly because—oh heavens, there was something rivetting about that man's hard and totally masculine good looks. Even more so here, under the softness of the artificial lights. In spite of her antagonism, she couldn't help staring at him.

He'd changed into a white collarless shirt and well-fitting dark pants and he looked very civilised and intimidatingly mature. Darryn had suddenly lost all her self-confidence. His silvery blue eyes were taking in the brilliance of her hair and she could practically see the workings of his mind. *It can't be real,* he was thinking, and she wanted to laugh. It was sheer nervousness, she knew. Then when his glance moved down the length of her slender body and came back to rest on her mouth, somehow she didn't want to laugh any more, though she didn't know why.

"You look as though you're going out to dinner, Darryn," he greeted her, smiling in a way that unsettled her even more than his easy use of her name. Anyone would think from his manner that they knew each other well. Yet they were strangers. And hostile strangers at that.

"Only on my own," Darryn heard herself say and was appalled. What had happened to the things she'd meant to tell him? They seemed to have gone right out of her head and she was furious with herself. She'd have to do better than this. Just because the man was good-looking, she wasn't going to behave like a—a star-struck teenager.

"You don't have a date then?" he half-stated, his smile deepening as did the look, intent and considering, that he was giving her.

"No. Do you?" she countered, and, remembering Mrs. Dwyer, automatically looked over his shoulder as if the woman might be looming up behind him.

"I was hoping to have dinner with you," he said. "Shall we discuss the possibility over a drink?"

She meant to say "No thank you," but instead she nodded helplessly, and before she knew what had happened, they were sitting at a low table in a secluded corner of the lounge and he was ordering drinks. If he'd asked her what she'd like, she wasn't aware of it. She was too shaken by her own incomprehensible behaviour to be rational.

All the same, she reassured herself, she might as well find out what this was all about. Because she couldn't even begin to make a guess. Frankly, she'd had the idea that he'd steer so clear of her and her camera and her blatant hints about visiting Moon Mountain that she'd never catch a glimpse of so much as one hair of his head again. And here he was, asking her to dine with him. She didn't imagine he was going to invite her to his cattle station, so he must want something, she concluded wryly. But what on earth could a man like Eyre Madison want from a girl like her?

She was soon to find out.

Chapter Two

"We were interrupted in the middle of our conversation this afternoon," he said a moment later, looking at her over his glass of scotch as she sipped her orange and vodka.

"Were we?" Darryn had the strange feeling she must be dreaming all this, it was so absurd. "I thought we'd both said all we had to say."

"Oh, I hardly think so," he said with a slight smile.

She hurried on, "I apologised for my blunder, and as far as I'm concerned there's nothing more to be said. Nothing of importance," she finished positively.

"No?" His blue eyes looked at her hard and in their depths she thought she saw a flicker of amusement. "Is your drink as you like it?"

"Yes, it's fine," she stammered, disconcerted and almost choking on a mouthful. She'd only ever had vodka and orange once before, and not being a connoisseur when it came to alcoholic drinks, she was inclined to be uncritical, providing what she was given didn't taste too potent.

"Good . . . Well then, I had the distinct impression you had something else on your mind quite apart from offering me an apology."

"Did you?" She was recovering her aplomb and was determined on steering a straight course—right between all the loaded questions he was putting to her. If he thought he was going to edge her into a repeat performance of this afternoon's conversation, for whatever reason, so she'd ask for another snub, then he had another think coming. "What could have given you that idea, I wonder?"

He raised one dark eyebrow and drained his glass. "You were telling me—of your own volition—about the assignment you've been given from Sydney. You seemed very enthusiastic about it."

"Oh that," she said with a shrug. "I didn't mean to bore you about that. It's of no interest to you."

"You're wrong," he said, setting his glass down and leaning towards her a little. "Publicity of any kind on this particular part of the outback is of considerable interest to me. I've been thinking about you, as a matter of fact, and I have a proposition to put to you."

Darryn stared at him, frowning. "What do you mean?"

"Briefly, that visit you're so anxious to make to Moon Mountain could be arranged," he said, his eyes intent on her face.

She moved her hand nervously and knocked over his empty glass.

"I don't particularly want to visit Moon Mountain, Mr. Madison," she said with an attempt at casualness. "As you reminded me this afternoon, there are plenty of other cattle stations around. I can manage to do my assignment without your—" She hesitated, rejected the word favours, and finished, "Your interference."

She saw anger deep in the blue of his eyes, but he didn't say whatever it was he probably felt like saying.

"So what you'll do is to race out somewhere on that motorcycle I saw you riding, take a quick look around some cattle station, click your camera in all directions, then career back to Alice before dark and try to make something of what's no more than nonsense."

Darryn opened her mouth to make a furious retort but he went on scathingly, "What kind of a record of outback life do you think you'll produce under those circumstances? It's laughable. For a girl who takes a pride in her work—takes herself seriously as a photographer."

"How do you know I do that?" she interrupted. She was uncomfortable about the lie she'd told him. She did want to make some sort of a record of outback life of course, but it would be a purely personal thing, and in any case, she'd never dream of attacking it in the way he'd suggested. She found his remarks offensive, and suspected he'd intended her to.

"Oh, I know," he said, his glance still intent. "I've been talking to Margo Talbot about you. She telephoned me after I got back to the hotel. To make the apologies that you'd already made. She told me you were beginning to distinguish yourself in Sydney—that you'd had photographs in a quite prestigious exhibition."

He paused, and Darryn felt embarrassed. She really hadn't made much of a mark.

"It rather made me wonder why you've come to bury yourself in the wild heart of this continent. Am I right in guessing it's the usual thing—a broken love affair?"

She shook her head. "I wanted to get away from the city, to see the real Australia—"

"That figures," he said with a slight smile. "Your position with Talbot Studios is only temporary, isn't it? In other words, it's fulfilling a useful purpose as far as you're concerned."

He seemed to have been finding out a lot of things about her from Margo, Darryn thought, and she wondered uncomfortably if he'd mentioned that fictitious assignment. She didn't know what Margo would have made of that, and only hoped she'd been discreet. As for his implication that she was making use of Margo, she wasn't going to put up with that.

"If Mrs. Talbot offers me a permanent position, I'll take it," she said coldly. "I happen to like living here."

His teeth flashed in a brief smile. "That's good to hear." He glanced at her empty glass. "Another drink? Or are you ready for dinner?"

"I didn't say I'd have dinner with you, Mr. Madison, and I don't want another drink. I'd rather hear what this proposition of yours is. Just out of curiosity," she added hastily, and clenched her fists when he laughed.

"I'll tell you over dinner," he said with a hard smile. "I don't want to rush you."

She stared at him frustratedly. He was too used to having his own way, she decided. Somehow, she hadn't acted at all as she'd meant to, and now he was trying to cash in on her curiosity and persuade her—force her, rather—to have dinner with him. Well, he could tell her here and now what his famous proposition was. She wasn't moving until she'd heard it.

"I'd rather you told me about it now," she said. "I'm not in a hurry. And I'm not in the habit of going out with strangers."

His mouth curved mockingly. "Darryn—this afternoon you practically invited yourself to my cattle station. Now you're quibbling at having dinner with me. It hardly makes sense, does it?"

"It does to me," she said, annoyed. "Besides, I didn't invite myself to your cattle station. I merely mentioned—"

She stopped, suddenly aware that she'd raised her voice and that a number of people were looking at them. And that Eyre Madison was getting exasperated with her. In a minute he'd walk out and leave her, and then she'd never know what his proposition was, and she'd never get to Moon Mountain. And she'd never forgive herself for *that*.

She pushed back her chair resignedly. "All right. I suppose I'll have dinner with you. I'm hungry, anyway. I apologise if I've been difficult."

"Oh, it's understandable. An empty stomach on top of too much rodeo plus the added complication of red hair," he said with a smile that got through to her in spite of his implied opinion of people with red hair. It wasn't really red, anyhow, but she wasn't going to argue that point. He could think what he liked, she decided, as she walked ahead of him towards the door.

In the narrow garden that separated the motel from the street, she paused. The air was warm, and above, in a cloudless sky, the silver moon floated, surrounded by the glitter of stars. How different it was from the sky in Sydney, Darryn reflected. The stars so bright, so close, the air so clean. She felt the soft night wind lift tendrils of hair from her neck like a caress and turned to look at the man who stood beside her, to find with a shock that he was looking down at her. His face was very dark, and in the moonlight the silvery blue of his eyes merged into mysterious shadow.

She moved abruptly, but when he took her arm she didn't pull away, and the touch of his fingers sent an oddly pleasurable shiver up and down her spine. They walked to his car in silence, and neither of them spoke as he drove to a restaurant that Darryn hadn't known existed. It was small and classy and discreet. There were hand-crocheted tablecloths on the softly lit tables, and the coolness of potted ferns around.

Without quite knowing why, Darryn looked about her quickly as she took her seat at the table they were shown to. She encountered the interested glances of several people whose faces she'd seen at the rodeo, and exchanged smiles with one or two of them. She didn't see Mrs. Dwyer, and with a feeling of relief brought her attention back to Eyre, who was studying the menu.

At his invitation, she helped him select their meal, and they settled for pâté with watercress, followed by beef bourguignon. Eyre ordered a bottle of red wine, and in spite of a slight feeling of uneasiness, Darryn enjoyed the meal, giving it her full attention. Her curiosity was almost killing her, but she refused to ask Eyre any questions about his mysterious proposition.

It was not until they were finishing their wine, with the cheese they'd mutually agreed on instead of a dessert, that he at last returned to the matter that was the main reason for their being here together.

"Darryn, I know you told me you don't particularly want to come to Moon Mountain, but in actual fact, it would please you to spend some time there, wouldn't it?"

In other words, he didn't believe what she'd said, she thought, still smarting from the snub she'd received out at the rodeo grounds. She debated how to answer him, and knew her reply hinged on how much she wanted to see Moon Mountain—the place where, had things been different, she would have spent most of her life to date.

"Well—I suppose I wouldn't mind," she admitted finally.

His mouth twisted. "You find it hard to be gracious, don't you? No one would ever guess I was offering to do you a favour."

"I don't accept favours from strangers," she said unwisely, and wasn't altogether surprised at his retort.

"Then you shouldn't angle for them. You were the one who let me know what you wanted. It was the reason behind your apology for infringing on my privacy, wasn't it?"

She flushed slightly. Maybe it was, but it was hardly tactful of him to point it up. Darryn sipped her wine and helped herself to cheese and told him pleasantly, "I don't ask for something a second time anyhow—not after it's been refused me."

"It's beneath your dignity, is it?" he commented. "Well, in this particular instance you don't have to ask for anything—it's being offered to you on a plate."

She raised her eyes to his. "I don't believe that. *You're* not offering me anything on a plate. Why should you? I wish you'd come to the point."

"Right. Then I'll do that," he said, his voice suddenly businesslike. "I want something of you. I want you to come to Moon Mountain as my visitor, to keep quiet about your photographic activities, and let it be understood you're around simply because you and I are attracted to each other."

"Attracted to each other?" Darryn blinked in surprise. A man like Eyre Madison attracted to her! "But—we're not."

"All right, we're not," he said crisply. "But it's quite possible to let it appear that way. From my point of view, I find you very appealing with that extraordinary hair and those engaging green eyes." His glance moved to her breast as if to indicate that she had other attractions as well, and then he went on dryly, "As for you, the possibility of marrying the boss of Moon Mountain might very well appeal to you."

"It might, but it doesn't," she retorted swiftly, pushing her glass away and leaning back in her chair. "I think the whole idea's preposterous, Mr. Madison. Particularly since you told me I *would* be able to take those photos. That's positively the only reason I could be at all interested."

"Oh, I'll make sure you can take all the pictures you want," he said impatiently. "I merely said you'd have to let it seem you were no more than an amateur photographer. That shouldn't be hard." He leaned across the table as he spoke, and took her hand possessively in his. Darryn's nerves tingled, but when she tried to snatch her hand away, she found she couldn't, because his fingers closed hard around her wrist.

"People are looking at us," she whispered angrily.

"I know," he whispered back mockingly. "It's part of the reason I brought you here—so we can be seen together. It will help to give credibility to the fact that I'm embarked on a love affair with a devastatingly attractive girl."

Me, Darryn thought, mentally reeling. She still hadn't the faintest clue what it was all about.

"But—why?" she asked, feeling as if she must have asked the same question at least a hundred times and never received a satisfactory answer. He'd released her hand now but she could still feel where his fingers had been, and she was conscious of the fact that their tête-à-tête was causing some interest. At least Mrs. Dwyer wasn't there, she thought rather ridiculously.

"I'll explain it all to you more fully later on," Eyre said, and the way he looked at her made her feel even more conspicuous. "For various reasons, I'm under some pressure from my family to marry. In fact, a suitable bride is being thrust down my throat. Well, a lesson must be taught. I'll marry in my own time, and I'll choose my own wife. To make my point quite unmistakably, I shall produce my own candidate. You," he added, narrowing his silver-blue eyes. "I think that puts you sufficiently in the picture, doesn't it, Darryn?"

Darryn didn't think so. "Why me?" she wanted to ask, but he'd think she was fishing for a compliment. She reached for her wine glass, looking across the table at him as she did so. He looked back at her unsmilingly and for a few mad seconds she seemed to forget what they were talking about and to lose herself completely in the fascination of his very male regard.

"Well?" he said, insistently.

Darryn swallowed, and unlocked her eyes from his with an effort. "What—what would I be expected to do?" she asked, knowing she was tempted against all reason by this proposition that was so odd and so suspect that if she had any sense she'd reject it at once.

"Nothing that need frighten the life out of you," he said with a mocking look. "Just be there—spend your time with me—give the general impression that you and I are pretty much absorbed in each other."

"But I couldn't do that," she objected.

"Of course you could," he averred. "It would be in the best interests of each of us to spend our time together." He looked at her quizzically, and Darryn knew he was waiting for her to give him her answer. Which, naturally enough, would be no. She'd have to be crazy, plain crazy, to agree to such an impossible condition . . .

"I don't think Mrs. Talbot would free me," she said stiffly.

"Ah, but she would," he contradicted her. "I've already looked into that. I—er—sounded her out this evening over the telephone, so you see everything is nicely teed up."

"I'll need time to think it over just the same, Mr. Madison," she said calmly, though inwardly she was not calm at all. Her hand shook as she reached for her glass and finished her wine.

"I want your answer now," he said flatly. "I'm leaving for Moon Mountain at eleven tomorrow, and either you come with me or you don't."

Darryn tried to think, but she found it impossible to make up her mind what to do. How on earth could she pretend that she and this man were attracted to each other? But on the other hand Moon Mountain had been a dream in her mind for a long time. . . . With sudden recklessness, she told him, "All right. I suppose I'll come."

"I thought you would," he said, and something in his tone seemed to suggest he'd known all along that he'd get what he wanted. Darryn immediately, and perversely, wished she'd refused to cooperate.

Not many minutes later he drove her back to her motel. But before she could get out of the car, he turned towards her and with a movement that was not to be resisted drew her into his arms and kissed her. She knew it was deliberate, that it meant nothing, yet to her annoyance it gave her a thrill all the same. She liked the feel of his mouth as it moved against hers, the firmness of his arm that held her to him, and when he let her go, her heart was beating rapidly.

"It's not going to be so hard to take is it, Darryn?" he murmured close to her ear.

She shrugged with a nonchalance she was far from feeling, and made her escape quickly.

In the motel room, she switched on the lights and put her hands to her cheeks. They felt hot, and she knew it was the wine and the kisses. Mostly the kisses. She felt oddly disturbed. What on earth was she letting herself in for? She suddenly realised there'd probably be some love-making attached to this adventure, Eyre Madison being the kind of man he was. She shouldn't have allowed him to kiss her, of course. That had been a mistake. Well, she'd soon let him know she found him far from irresistible.

Maybe she wouldn't even go, she thought as she slid into bed.

But when she woke in the morning after a surprisingly undisturbed sleep, she knew she wasn't going to break her promise. She had to weigh what he wanted from her against what *she* wanted from Moon Mountain, and she'd keep that in the forefront of her mind.

Feeling unusually cheerful, she showered and dressed, and decided to go to the studio to check with

Margo that it was all right for her to take a few days off. But at the back of her mind, she knew she was hoping to find out something more about that man . . .

"Well, hello!" Margo greeted her brightly as she came in. "I hoped you might pop in for a minute before you left for Moon Mountain. Did Eyre Madison catch up with you all right last night?" she added with a rather knowing smile.

"Yes. I had dinner with him," Darryn admitted. She wondered exactly what Eyre had told Margo, if Margo knew everything. The thought made her blood freeze, but she discarded it instantly. Eyre wouldn't have told anyone of the bargain he planned to strike with her.

"You're a lucky girl," Margo went on. "And a very clever one, to have told Eyre all about this marvellous project you mean to work on. You didn't tell *me* about it."

Darryn stared at her. It wasn't hard to guess what Margo was thinking, but she was quite wrong. She certainly hadn't angled for that invitation because she found Eyre attractive.

"I'm sorry," she murmured. "I meant to leave it till later. But when this opportunity came up I—I took it. I won't go if you'd rather I didn't, of course."

Margo looked at her hard for a moment and then relaxed into a smile.

"No, my dear, I wouldn't dream of standing in your way. Besides, Eyre's already persuaded me. Take all the time you like. You know I'm not urgently in need of an assistant, that I promised to take you on mainly to please June. A week or so doesn't matter."

A week or so! A couple of days, more likely, Darryn thought. By then, she and Eyre would have had quite enough of each other, and his family would accept that he wasn't going to marry this other girl.

"Oh, I shan't stay away long, Margo," she insisted.

"I can take all the pictures I want in a couple of days. But I do appreciate your letting me go, especially after that stupid mistake I made yesterday. Taking that photo, I mean. I didn't know the man was Eyre Madison, and I was quite sure Mrs. Dwyer wanted it. She's very pretty, isn't she?"

"Very pretty," Margo agreed. "She's a—er— particular friend of Eyre's. Unfortunately, she's married to a man much older than herself. A station owner. His property adjoins Moon Mountain. It's not a happy marriage, and Harry is a very sick man. In fact," she added, lowering her voice, "he's just about on his last legs. So you can understand it would look really bad for Ellen and Eyre to be photographed together at the rodeo."

Darryn's eyes had widened. "Do you mean she and Eyre are—that there's something between them?" she asked hesitantly.

Margo nodded.

"I mean exactly that, though it's not generally known. They've been very discreet. But I've known Ellen for a long time, and she confides in me. I wouldn't have breathed a word of it to you except that Eyre's invited you to Moon Mountain, and I wouldn't like you to get the wrong idea."

"You needn't worry," Darryn said decidedly. "I'm not likely to do that." It shocked her a little to know that Eyre was having an affair with a woman whose husband was so ill. No wonder he'd been furious about her taking that photo! She could see, too, why he was annoyed at being pressured into marrying someone else, and was confusing the issue by inviting her to Moon Mountain. But understanding it didn't make the facts any more palatable.

"I'm relieved to hear it," Margo was saying. "I should have known you'd have more sense than to set

your sights on someone like Eyre Madison. He's very
attractive, isn't he?"

She looked at Darryn and rolled her eyes, and
Darryn smiled and murmured, "I suppose so."

"Now come along and we'll have a cup of coffee,"
Margo suggested. "I put some on to percolate just
before you arrived. We can talk about your visit to the
Madisons while we drink it."

Darryn followed her out to the kitchenette. She
didn't like gossip, but all the same she hoped that
Margo would have something to say about the Madisons of Moon Mountain. After all, forewarned was
forearmed, she told herself.

"I'm going to give you some advice, Darryn," Margo
said presently as they took their coffee through to the
studio. "You're very young and I know too much about
Eyre Madison and his charms not to be just a little
concerned about you. He's—susceptible, shall we say,
and I daresay he's finding it hard waiting for the woman
he loves to be free. So darling, you really mustn't take
it seriously if he flirts with you. You're an exceptionally
pretty girl and you're bound to be thrown together at
least a little in a place as isolated as Moon Mountain. In
fact, anything could happen. If you allow it to. My
advice to you is to hang on to your head and your
heart."

Darryn lowered her lashes, remembering Eyre's kiss
and her response, remembering his "proposition," and
knowing that they were going to be thrown together
more than a little.

"Don't worry," she said lightly. "I'm definitely not
going to Moon Mountain with romance in mind."

"I'm glad." Margo smiled. "I believe the jackeroo is
a very pleasant young man, but you'll probably find old
Kate Madison rather too much for you! I've never met
her, but from the stories I've heard she must be a very

intimidating old lady. She used to run the station before Eyre took over, and I believe she did it very efficiently. Just as well as any man, in fact."

"Did she really?" Darryn murmured. That must have been at the time when her mother was at Moon Mountain, she thought, recalling one or two remarks her mother had made. It sounded very much as though this old lady was one of the relatives who were so keen for Eyre to make a suitable marriage. She rather thought she'd get the steely eye and she didn't look forward to it.

"She'll very quickly make mincemeat out of you if she suspects you have ideas about Eyre," Margo remarked, more or less confirming her thoughts. "The Madisons were a snobbish lot in the old days, and though times have changed I guess it's all still there, simmering away gently under the surface and ready to burst forth if there's sufficient provocation."

"Oh dear," Darryn said dismayed. "I'm beginning to wish I hadn't said I'd go. A mere junior photographer's not going to be given much of a welcome." And neither was the daughter of a stockman who'd once worked at Moon Mountain, she reflected. Quite likely, if her parentage was known, she wouldn't be welcomed at all.

"Don't worry, they'll be gracious," Margo assured her. "After all, you'll be Eyre's guest. I'm sure you'll enjoy yourself vastly if you remember my advice. It will be an experience you'll remember all your life."

Darryn was sure it would be, though for reasons rather different from those Margo had in mind.

A little later, after refusing another cup of coffee, she said she must go. She had her packing to do, and she wanted to be ready when Eyre came for her.

"I feel mean leaving you to deal with all the rodeo pictures," she remarked, but Margo shrugged it off.

"My dear, I've been dealing with this kind of thing single-handed for years. It's true I'm looking forward to relaxing a little more in the near future, but I wouldn't dream of holding you up. Run along and enjoy yourself. Let me know how things are going. I suppose you'll be writing to your parents with the news."

Darryn nodded and smiled, but she doubted whether she'd let her mother know she was going to Moon Mountain. Not yet, anyhow. Her mother preferred to forget the brief period of her life that had been spent on a cattle station.

Well before eleven o'clock she was ready and waiting, her motel bill settled, her luggage neatly packed, a stack of film packed away in her big zippered carry bag. She was feeling excited by now, and her mind churned with curiosity about the people at Moon Mountain. She knew that the Madisons must have been there in her mother's day, because of what Margo had said about Kate. As she waited for Eyre in the motel lounge, she recalled things her mother had said years ago, when she'd pestered her to tell her about her father, and about the cattle station with the romantic name.

"Darryn, I was there only a few weeks and I hated it. I spent all my time sitting alone inside a little bungalow, crying and wishing I was back home again."

"Yes, but what was so *bad* about it?" Darryn had persisted. "Was it my father?"

"Oh, there was nothing bad about Chris. He was a good-looking man with dark hair and eyes that tilted up like yours. He loved the outback, but it bored me to tears. I hated the heat, the roughness. And the raw meat! I'd never had to cut up meat till then, never even had to cook a steak. I was little more than a schoolgirl and used to being taken care of. The boss was a woman—the men called her the Missus. She wore riding breeches and a man's hat and carried a stockwhip."

That, Darryn knew now, had been Kate Madison.

Her mother said she'd never spoken to her, never invited her to the homestead, because she was "only a stockman's wife."

"It hurt my pride, being ignored," her mother had remembered. "I'd always had a lot of notice taken of me because I was quite brilliant at school. That was part of the trouble. I was sick of study and the tameness of my parents' lifestyle. I wanted to live! But the fact was, I wasn't ready to be a wife, particularly not a stockman's wife."

Eventually, she'd run away from Moon Mountain—hidden in some traveller's car and gone back to Sydney to attend university, as her parents had always wanted her to do. And then discovered she was pregnant.

It must have been a shock, Darryn thought now, getting up from her chair and walking restlessly across the deserted lounge. She hadn't wanted a child of course, and she hadn't let Darryn's father know about it. Her parents had taken care of her, and later they'd looked after Darryn. Her father hadn't known of her existence until years later when the divorce was being instigated. What had become of him? Darryn wondered. Deep in her heart she was hurt that he'd never tried to contact her.

Yet she still had this strange feeling that she was more his daughter than she was her mother's, that the outback was where she belonged.

As for Moon Mountain, right now she discovered that she was a little bit afraid of going there. But that was because of the complication of her agreement with Eyre Madison.

Chapter Three

Eyre arrived at the motel on the dot of eleven. He greeted Darryn as casually as if they were old friends, his glance flicking quickly over the pale green cotton shirt and matching below-the-knee-length knickers she was wearing, then coming to rest on her shining red-gold hair. Its curly length heaped up and caught neatly by two greenish pearl-shell combs, a present from her grandmother who had brought them back from Lord Howe Island years ago.

While he was checking her over, she took the opportunity of doing the same to him, and she approved reluctantly of what he wore—a short-sleeved safari suit in a colour that Darryn designated as celadon. Her eyes were drawn compulsively to the sensational silver streak in his slightly ruffled smoke-brown hair, and she wondered what had put it there—whether it was something to do with his frustrated love affair with Ellen Dwyer.

He met her eyes, intercepting her examination of him, and smiled slightly; Darryn looked away hurriedly and walked ahead of him out of the motel. She envied him his poise and wished she could feel as sure of herself. Right at this moment she wasn't looking forward to the long drive to Moon Mountain, alone with him. Quite positively she'd stay no longer than a few days, she promised herself. That much of his company wasn't going to kill her anyhow.

She'd thought last night that the car he drove was an old one, but by daylight it looked practically a wreck, and her heart sank. Imagine bumping over the rough outback roads in that! It was going to be a long and gruelling drive for sure. But she wasn't her father's daughter if the mere thought of that intimidated her. She opened the door on the passenger's side and climbed in while Eyre disposed of her luggage. By the time he took his seat behind the wheel she was looking bright and carefree.

But he was too observant and as they drove out of town he told her, "This is a hired car, by the way, so you can relax and take that rather fixed smile off your face. We'll be flying to Moon Mountain. Does that make you feel better?"

"Well—yes," she admitted. "Not that I mind a long car ride."

His smile was mocking. "We'll save that for another time, then."

Such as when I'm leaving, she thought, and some stockman's delegated to return me to Alice Springs.

He'd said last night that he'd explain everything to her later on, but he told her nothing as they drove out to the airfield. He asked if she had plenty of film, and whether she intended taking black and white or colour shots, and she talked animatedly about that for a few minutes. By that time, they'd reached the airfield, so she'd have to ask her questions in the plane.

She loved the flight over the shimmering land that was the very heart of the outback. From the air, it looked fantastic with its deeply shadowed gorges cut into the red ancient earth, its vast stretches of semi-desert, of spinifex; its barren wastes where it looked as if no one and nothing could survive.

But the realisation that soon Moon Mountain would be coming into view reminded her that Eyre had still told her nothing, and she turned to him with determination. "Mr. Madison—before we land—I must know one or two things. This other girl—will she be there?"

He glanced sideways at her, raising one dark eyebrow.

"For heaven's sake, stop calling me Mr. Madison. Eyre—darling—anything but that." He smiled mockingly at the expression that had come over her face. "Cyrilla won't be at Moon Mountain yet, and with luck her visit will be cancelled. *And* the party I suspect Ruth's planning to celebrate an engagement."

"You mean yours," Darryn said. "Well, it all sounds very odd to me. I mean—you're not exactly the kind of man who lets other people tell him what to do. So why—" She paused, glanced at him and found his face was impassive, and felt infuriated. "Look—if you're not going to tell me anything, you can't expect me to cooperate."

She saw him frown, and the corner of his mouth tilt upwards. "You're typically female, aren't you, Darryn? You're quite right, by the way, about my not liking to be told what I'm to do. That's the crux of the matter. But since I'm considered to have an unromantic view of marriage, all this business has been arranged by my aunt, Ruth Nash, in the hope of hustling me into it. The chief reason being that Kate, my grandmother, has shown signs lately of not being quite her usual hearty self. Ruth thinks it's time she moved to Adelaide to live with her, and be properly looked after. But my wonderful grandmother is a very stubborn old lady." He smiled slightly. "For years she's sworn that she's not

moving from Moon Mountain until she's been to my
wedding. Hence the plots and plans."

"But if she's not well," Darryn objected, "shouldn't
you—"

"Shouldn't I rush off and marry someone immediately? Is that what you're thinking?"

"Of course not," Darryn said coldly. "But I don't
imagine your aunt just plucked someone out of the air,
did she?"

"Not exactly. I've known Cyrilla for several years,"
he admitted. "She's a friend of one of my sisters, and I
saw quite a lot of her recently in Adelaide, one way and
another. But when I decide to marry, I'll set things in
motion myself. If you're worried about my grandmother, you needn't be. I'm fond of Kate. I won't let her
come to any harm. Meanwhile, your appearance at
Moon Mountain is going to foul up the lines very
effectively. Is all that too much for you to absorb, or do
you get the general idea?"

"More or less," Darryn said slowly. It had suddenly
occurred to her that of course it would make sense for
Eyre to marry Ellen Dwyer. For the "unromantic"
reason that the Dwyer property would then be added to
Moon Mountain. All the same, he must be in love with
her as well. Margo Talbot had certainly given that
impression, and Mrs. Dwyer was a very attractive lady.

"Great," Eyre was saying. "Then I can depend on
you?"

"I suppose so," she said with a shrug.

A cluster of buildings had come into sight on the
ground below, and Eyre was bringing the plane gently
down to a small airstrip some distance away. Darryn
saw a vehicle race along a track that snaked out from
the buildings in their oasis of trees, and guessed it was
someone coming to meet them.

"Who's that?" she asked curiously.

"The jackeroo, Andrew McDonald, I should imagine," Eyre said carelessly.

"Oh!" Darryn exclaimed. "I've heard he's rather nice."

"Nice or not, you'll keep your eyes off him," Eyre said. "Just remember you're supposed to be my property."

Darryn bristled at the phrase. She told him curtly, "I'm not used to acting as if I were anyone's property. If that's what you want, you should have given me a few lessons before you brought me here."

"There was hardly time, was there?" he said sardonically. "But don't worry, Darryn. Once we're down on the ground again you can have all the lessons you like."

"Actually, I wouldn't *like* to have any," she told him acidly.

"Well, please yourself. But just keep it in mind that we're madly in love with each other. Okay?"

"Okay," she agreed and felt her heart thudding. She didn't think she was going to be desperately keen on playing this part. Besides, did it have to be as definite as that? Madly in love! It was expecting rather a lot, merely in return for allowing her to take a few photographs. However, she had her own reasons for wishing to visit his cattle station, and she'd do her bit and try not to cheat him—as long as he didn't carry things too far. In that case, she would disappear.

She glanced at him covertly and felt her nerve-ends tingle at the sight of his strong masculine profile. As Margo had said, he had a lot of charm, and she supposed most girls in her position would be falling over themselves to please him. But not Darryn Ross! She knew rather more than he thought about his marriage plans, unromantic or otherwise. Besides, she didn't like men who were so dictatorial, and she hadn't liked being snubbed either, when she'd angled for an

invitation. Even though she'd eventually got her invitation, it was only because it had suited him to give
it—with plenty of strings attached!

But wouldn't he be put out if he knew he was giving
house-guest status to the daughter of a former stockman! She caught her lower lip between her teeth to
hold back a nervous laugh. This whole project of
coming to the Northern Territory was turning out
unexpectedly different from anything she'd anticipated.
Even this pilgrimage to Moon Mountain where she had
her beginnings—somewhere deep in her heart she was
afraid it might all prove to be no more than a romantic
dream, that the reality would be anticlimactic.

Well, she could still take photographs, and as well as
that there was the crazy pact she'd made with Eyre
Madison. Somehow or other she had to fulfill that, and
she only hoped it wouldn't prove to be too much of an
ordeal.

A few minutes later, he'd brought the little aircraft
down neatly and Darryn clambered out. Eyre unloaded
the luggage, and a young man with dark hair and an
olive complexion strolled over from the dusty car that
was pulled up in the shade of some eucalyptuses.

"Hello!" he exclaimed, his brown eyes roaming over
Darryn in obvious appreciation. "This is a pleasant
surprise. I didn't know anyone was coming back with
you, Eyre."

"I'm aware of that," Eyre said quizzically. Then,
turning to Darryn, he said, "Darling, this is Andrew
McDonald, the jackeroo. Andrew—Darryn Ross."

Darryn, who had blinked with shock at the endear-
ment, swallowed hard, and somehow managed to smile
and to murmur, "Hello." She wondered what else Eyre
would say about her, but apparently the jackeroo didn't
rate any explanations, for he merely continued, "Give
me a hand with this luggage, will you, Andy, and we'll
get moving. I guess it must be lunchtime."

Darryn was allocated to the back seat, and Eyre sat beside the driver. "How's my grandmother?" she heard him ask as they started back along the double red track in the direction of the trees that completely hid the station buildings from sight.

"Mrs. Madison's okay. Better than when you went away. Though complaining she feels a little dizzy this morning."

"I hope that's not because I'm coming home," Eyre said dryly. "But perhaps a little company will liven her up."

The jackeroo didn't answer, and catching his eye in the rear-vision mirror, Darryn knew he was speculating about her. She'd have to be prepared for more of that once they reached the homestead, and she wondered how Eyre would introduce her. He could hardly present her as his fiancée, and she suspected he might simply allow the obvious conclusion to be drawn from their actions.

They'd all have to be *his* actions, she assured herself, because she wouldn't, *couldn't* act as if she were madly in love with him. She'd have to school herself not to flinch when he called her darling, but that was the mere tip of the iceberg, and she quailed at the thought of what other demonstrations of his affection she might have to suffer.

The homestead came fully into sight as they reached the end of a red gravel drive. It was a long low building, built in an L shape, its wide verandahs and its green painted roof shaded by tall gums and Indian rain trees. Darryn, climbing nervously out of the car, heard the hum of a generator and the screeching of white cockatoos as they flew overhead against the cloudless blue sky.

No one had come bursting out of the house to welcome them, thank goodness, though common sense told her it was only putting off the evil hour. Pretending to a lot more assurance than she felt, she moved towards the steps while the men dealt with the luggage. Andrew leaped gallantly ahead to open the door for her, and smiled down into her eyes as she passed him. She smiled back, but only fleetingly. As Eyre had warned her, she wasn't here to flirt with the jackeroo.

On the verandah, she waited for Eyre, and tried to pretend she wasn't nervous. All the same, she jumped slightly as he dropped the suitcase he was carrying and draped an arm around her shoulders. At the same instant, she realised that a woman had appeared from inside the house.

"Ruth—I've brought a visitor," Eyre said, his voice pleasant but firm. "Darling—this is my aunt, Ruth Nash, who's staying with us for a few weeks. This is Darryn Ross, Ruth." He pulled Darryn against him as he spoke, and she knew that was deliberate. It told his aunt what he hadn't put into words, and Darryn bit her lip at the fleeting and quickly suppressed expression on the other woman's face. Surprise? Outrage? Darryn wasn't sure, but it was gone, and blue eyes almost the same colour as Eyre's, but not nearly so striking against a fair skin, smiled at her.

"Well, this is a surprise! We weren't expecting you, Darryn. My nephew is inclined to act on impulse. . . . Come along inside. I'm sure you must be ready for some lunch. Have you come far today?"

"Just from Alice Springs," Darryn said, trying out a shy smile and hoping it didn't look coy. Eyre had released her and she was being ushered graciously enough into the house. She wished desperately that she could have said that she was working as a photographer in Alice Springs and that Mr. Madison had very kindly invited her to stay for a few days so that she could take some photographs, but of course that was out of the question.

"Eyre—you'd better go in and see Mother. She hasn't made up her mind whether or not to join us for lunch, but she probably will now we have a visitor."

The wire door closed softly.

"Now let's see where we can settle you," Ruth Nash said, her voice gracious but just a little cool, or so it seemed to Darryn's oversensitive ears. "We're expecting another guest later on. Though you may have gone before she comes."

"I'm afraid I'm being a nuisance," Darryn said evasively, as she followed the older woman along a side passage. She felt it was up to Eyre, not her, to indicate how long she'd be staying. And personally, she hoped it would be no longer than a few days.

"This is a lovely room," Ruth said, opening a door. "It misses the afternoon sun so it's cool at night. . . . Of course you're not being a nuisance, Darryn. This is Eyre's home, not mine, you know. I'm only a visitor here these days. My home is in Adelaide with my husband."

She glanced round the room and crossed to the bed to see if it was made up, and Darryn studied her swiftly. She was a slender woman in her early fifties, with beautifully styled and cut silver hair, high cheekbones and intensely blue eyes.

She turned suddenly to smile at Darryn but it was a very cool smile, and Darryn could understand why. Eyre had certainly sprung a surprise in bringing an unknown girl home to Moon Mountain.

"I shan't have to bother the girls, the bed's made up. Would you like to freshen up before you come in to lunch? Andrew will bring your suitcase along presently, but your unpacking can wait an hour or so, can't it? I'm sure you must be hungry."

Oh dear, she was being so polite, even though she'd suggested that Darryn's visit was going to be a very short one. She showed her where the bathroom was, gave her instructions as to how to get to the dining room, then left her to herself.

Darryn looked round the room curiously. It was big and spacious with an unexpectedly modern built-in wardrobe painted ivory to match the walls. There was a matching dressing table with a big wall mirror over it, and as well there were two light and airy Perspex tables—one accommodating a reading lamp—and two marvellously comfortable-looking cushioned chairs. The bed was large, definitely made for two, and covered with a cotton bedspread made of the same material as the curtains at the long windows—pale water-green, patterned with tiny flowers.

Darryn headed for the bathroom, and found it as modern as the bedroom, in sparkling white and blue. How long would Ruth Nash's politeness last, she wondered, once Eyre started putting on his act of being madly in love with her? She knew she was in a very doubtful position, and heaven knew what Kate Madison was going to think of her. And—ghastly thought— if all that was wanted was for Eyre to marry, wasn't it just possible the old lady might decide that she'd "do?" That a bird in the hand was worth two in the bush?

Drying her hands on the guest towel that lay folded on top of a white enamelled cabinet, she grimaced at her reflection. She didn't really think she'd be accepted so easily by a woman like Kate Madison. It was much more likely, as Margo had said, that Kate would make mincemeat out of her. And that, though unpleasant, would, in the long run, be a whole lot more tolerable than the alternative.

She was in the bedroom brushing out her hair at the mirror when Eyre brought her suitcase in and set it down on one of the Perspex tables.

"Everything all right—darling?" he asked, raising one eyebrow. His eyes moved over her, lingering on her loosened hair, its red-gold bright against her pale skin. "I've been in to see Kate—my grandmother. She's decided she's going to join us for lunch—she's looking forward to meeting you."

Darryn swallowed. What had he told *her?* she wondered anxiously. That they were in love? It was really crazy . . . "Well, I'm not looking forward to meeting *her,*" she said, then turned away from the look in his eyes as he watched her through the mirror. She pushed up her hair quickly, and reached for one of her pearl-shell combs. "I don't know how I'm going to cope with all these relatives of yours. Particularly Ka—your grandmother."

"Oh?" He moved closer to her and took hold of her wrist, drawing her hand against his chest. Her hair fell down about her face, and she felt with a curious shock the warmth of his body through his cotton jacket. "Kate's not going to eat you."

"Isn't she?" she asked, disturbed by the pressure of his fingers on her flesh. "That's not what I heard."

He looked at her hard.

"What *did* you hear? And from whom?"

She didn't answer. Instead, she tried to wrench her hand away from him, though to her fury without success.

"Let me fix my hair—they'll be waiting for us to come to lunch."

"Let them wait," he said inexorably, and this time, instead of simply holding onto her hand, he slipped his arms around her and pulled her against him, looking down into her face. "Now are you going to answer my question? Who's been talking to you about my family and my grandmother?"

"Does it matter?" she asked, forcing herself not to struggle, but very conscious of the contact between their two bodies and of the increased rate of her heart beat. "I don't need anyone to tell me that I'm hardly suitable house-guest material for the Madisons of Moon Mountain."

"What's that supposed to mean?" he asked angrily. "That we're snobs? Or that you have a low opinion of yourself for some reason? That's not the impression you've given me to date. You're brim-full of self-confidence from what I've seen of you. I'm sure you're quite able to cope with whatever comes up. I wouldn't have invited you along if I'd thought otherwise."

He tangled his fingers in her hair and tilted her face up to his, and their eyes met. She found herself totally unable to look away as he seemed to search for what was in her mind. She had no idea what he read in her eyes, and at that moment she didn't really know what she was thinking herself. She only knew that she was increasingly aware of the intimate way he was holding her, and that her heart was pounding as if—something was going to happen . . .

Steps sounded in the hallway outside, and she whispered agitatedly, "Let me go—please—" Instead, he lowered his head and his mouth sought hers, and he was kissing her passionately when Ruth spoke from the doorway.

"Oh . . . excuse me. I came to see if Darryn was ready to join us for lunch." Her voice was cool, and Darryn knew her face was flushed as Eyre loosened his hold on her and looked down at her quizzically.

"No, I don't think she's quite ready, Ruth," he said, his mouth curling up at one corner. "Don't wait for us. We'll be along." He scooped Darryn's hair back from her face with his two hands, brushing his fingers intimately against her hot cheeks. "We'd better get your hair up again, darling."

Writhing inwardly, Darryn reached for her brush, and after a moment, Ruth vanished.

Darryn looked at Eyre angrily.

"You did all that deliberately, didn't you?"

"Of course," he agreed. "You surely weren't surprised—you know why I invited you here."

Darryn wanted to stamp her foot. It was all so idiotic. She wished she could do as he was doing, and view the whole thing lightly and impersonally. Why couldn't she? she wondered frantically, as she fixed her hair with fingers that trembled and he stood, arms folded, watching her through half-closed eyes. How much easier it would be if she could play along with him, make a game of it. The trouble was, she was so inexperienced and he was quite the opposite. And then there was Ellen Dwyer. Though exactly what Ellen Dwyer had to do with the present situation, she didn't really know.

She finished fastening her hair, then used her lipstick, and wished that Eyre wouldn't watch her that way. Just as if they were—engaged or something.

Almost as though he'd read her thoughts, he turned away and moved towards the door, and after a moment she followed him.

Her first meeting with Kate Madison turned out to be less of an ordeal than she'd anticipated, possibly because the jackeroo sat at the lunch table with the family.

Kate Madison didn't look in the least intimidating. In fact, she looked so frail at first glance that Darryn simply couldn't imagine her riding around the property cracking a stockwhip and issuing orders. She was small, slight and silver-haired; there was a strong physical resemblance between herself and her daughter. But the old lady's skin was darker than Ruth's, weather-worn and wrinkled, and those silver-blue eyes were almost as stunning in her old lined face as Eyre's were against his dramatic darkness. It was the directness of her gaze that made Darryn realise that she was still a woman of strong character.

"So you're Darryn Ross," she remarked when Eyre

introduced them. "Well, we always welcome visitors here. I hope you'll enjoy yourself, Darryn—sure to, with two good-looking men to dance attendance on you."

"Thank you," Darryn murmured. She glanced at Eyre from under her lashes and encountered his sardonic smile. He knew, and she knew, that only one man would be dancing attendance on Darryn Ross.

An aboriginal woman in a blue cotton dress had brought in dishes of meat and salad, and gone silently away after one shy look at Darryn from huge limpid brown eyes. Ruth urged Darryn to help herself, the meal began, and questions were asked. Not of Darryn, but of Eyre. About his stay in Alice Springs, the success of the rodeo, who he'd seen there.

"And Ellen Dwyer?"

Darryn felt her heart give a guilty leap as Ruth spoke, and stared down at her plate as Eyre answered the question smoothly.

"Yes. Ellen was there. Looking very relaxed and enjoying her outing."

"I'm so glad. Harry must be getting back on his feet again, and that's a comforting thought. He can be such a nice man."

Eyre didn't comment, and the conversation switched to a more general topic. Darryn only half-listened. Ruth obviously didn't know how ill Harry Dwyer was. Nor did she know that it was because of Ellen that she, Darryn, was here now, protecting Eyre from being coupled off with some girl who was considered suitable for a man with an unromantic view of matrimony, saving him for Ellen Dwyer, in fact.

She thrust the thought to the back of her mind, her eyes roving round the long narrow dining-room with its wide glass doors opening onto a verandah that was green with indoor plants. The dining room furniture was old and traditional and of obviously good quality, yet if the house had a character, it was, curiously, one of self-effacement. As if the people living there now were more important than the past.

How could you get that sort of thing across in a photograph? It would be an interesting exercise, she thought, looking round the table and trying to decide who would best fit into the picture she was composing in her mind. Two people probably, and Kate would be one of them.

"We must think of some way of entertaining you this afternoon, Darryn," Ruth said, breaking in on her thoughts. "Perhaps you'd like to go out with Andrew and see something of the property."

"I'll be in that," the jackeroo exclaimed enthusiastically.

Darryn didn't know what to say. She looked helplessly in Eyre's direction. He was talking to Kate, but he'd heard what was being said and now he broke off to tell Ruth abruptly, "I'll look after Darryn. Andrew has work to do."

Andrew grimaced, and Darryn glanced quickly away.

"I'm sure you have things to see to as well, Eyre," Ruth said brightly. "If Darryn is interested, I can take her out for a drive in one of the cars. I have time to spare now Mother's feeling better."

"Don't think of it," Eyre said dryly. "Darryn will enjoy herself a whole lot more in my company, I assure you." Darryn quailed as he went on crisply, "Believe me, Ruth, I'm quite capable of seeing to the entertainment of my guests without your help. Nor do I need you to jog my elbow when it comes to managing this cattle station."

Ruth's face flushed darkly, and she pushed back her chair. "I apologise," she said stiffly. "I was only trying to be helpful. Excuse me, please." She left the room obviously very much put out, and after a moment there was a general movement from the table.

Everyone must be wondering about her, Darryn thought uncomfortably, but she didn't think Eyre intended to leave them in doubt for long. And while she was sorry for Ruth's being put in her place, she'd more or less asked for it. She was going to be made to take Darryn seriously whether she liked it or not, and Darryn wondered whether even now she could be considering putting off Cyrilla's visit.

As she followed Kate out of the dining room, she thought, not for the first time, that she'd been mad to get involved with the Madisons. And particularly with Eyre.

Chapter Four

"See you later, everyone," Andrew said cheerily outside the dining room. He winked at Darryn and strode off, and for just an instant she wished she could go with him.

A moment later Eyre put an arm carelessly round her shoulders as he asked Kate, "Are you going to take a rest, Kate? I must say you look all right to me—marvellous in fact, sparking on all four."

"I am sparking on all four. And I'm not going to take a rest. I'm going to sit on the verandah and talk to Darryn."

"Fine," Eyre said equably, taking no notice of the wildly imploring look Darryn sent him. "You can have exactly a quarter of an hour."

Darryn wanted to scream with rage and frustration as she went reluctantly onto the verandah, where Eyre settled Kate in her chair and then disappeared. Darryn sat down too, and steeled herself for the ordeal to come.

First she had to suffer a long slow scrutiny that began with her red-gold hair, continued to the tip of her sandalled feet and ended with a raising of narrowed eyes to her own.

"Well, Darryn Ross, I've never heard Eyre speak of you. You can't have known him very long. Where did you meet?"

"In Alice Springs," Darryn said uneasily. She fiddled with one of her hair combs, and it slid out of her hair onto her lap.

"At the rodeo?" Kate Madison reached for a wooden fan that lay on the cane table and began fanning herself gently, and Darryn caught the elusive fragrance of sandalwood. She felt gauche and inadequate as she thrust the comb back into her hair, while the old lady watched her coolly and finally repeated inexorably, "Well? Is that right? You met Eyre at the rodeo?"

How on earth was she supposed to answer a question like that? And why wasn't Eyre here to fence with this persistent old lady? Darryn gritted her teeth and asked innocently, "Didn't Eyre tell you?"

"Would I be asking you if he had?" Kate said acidly. "I'm just trying to get to the bottom of what I find incomprehensible behaviour. I'm going to be tactless and tell you that Eyre's invited another girl to Moon Mountain."

"I don't think that's really so," Darryn contradicted coolly. "Eyre told me it was you and Mrs. Nash who'd invited Cyrilla here. And if by his incomprehensible behaviour you mean asking me to Moon Mountain, then you'd better ask Eyre about that, Mrs. Madison, not me."

"I certainly intend doing that," the old lady snapped. "But be very sure, miss, it's Eyre that Cyrilla Goddard is coming here to see, not me. Have you thought of that?"

She put her nose in the air, fanned herself vigorously, and proceeded to ignore Darryn, who sat fuming inwardly, hating Eyre for getting her mixed up in what was none of her business.

Just when she thought she could stand the tension no longer, Kate addressed her again.

"You may think me an interfering and inquisitive old lady, Darryn, but Eyre is my only grandson, the last male in the Madison line. These things matter to me, though you may be one of those people to whom tradition and family mean nothing. Moon Mountain has been part of my life ever since I married into the Madison family when I was eighteen years old. I learned to love it then and I love it still. And I've expressed some of that love in sheer hard work."

Darryn nodded. I know, she thought. You rode around cracking your stockwhip and ignoring the stockmen's wives.

"My husband had a stroke, and my only son—Eyre's father—died," Kate continued. "I ran the station myself until Eyre was old enough to help me. I learned a great many things in those six years. One was that if you have a stud bull worth thousands of dollars, you select your breeding cows with care." She looked hard at Darryn, a faint glimmer of amusement in her bright blue eyes. "And so you see, it's very important to me what Eyre does with his life and who he marries."

Darryn bit her lip. "Yes, I see," she murmured, and said no more. Not for anything on earth was she going to get embroiled in a conversation about marriage, or about stud bulls and breeding cows. Eyre wasn't going to marry her, and she wished to heaven he'd told this imperious old lady that he intended to marry Ellen Dwyer.

"So here I am and here I intend to stay until Eyre has arranged his life on Moon Mountain to my satisfaction," Kate Madison went on. "My daughter wants me to pack up and go to Adelaide where she can look after me in my old age, but I have a duty to the future generations of Madisons and I'm not going to shirk it.

Think hard before you begin to get any romantic ideas about Eyre, Darryn Ross. If the outback's in your blood, that's a help. But you're from the city, aren't you?"

Darryn stared back at her. Yes, she was from the city, but what would Kate Madison say if she were to tell her, "I was conceived right here at Moon Mountain. But don't worry, I don't have any romantic ideas about your grandson. I wouldn't marry him in a fit."

She would have loved to make some such retort, instead of sitting here being lectured as if she were a nonentity. But a nonentity was undoubtedly what Kate Madison would consider the daughter of a stockman. Darryn Ross, in fact, hadn't a hope in the world of being selected as a breeding cow.

She swallowed down a nervous laugh, and ignoring the question she'd been asked, told Kate, "I'm sure I'll manage to work it all out without your help, Mrs. Madison. Besides, don't you think Eyre's rather too old to need a—guardian angel?"

The old lady gave her a sharp look. "No one's too old for that, Darryn. Or are you telling me that you are wiser than I am?"

Darryn shook her head. "I'm sorry," she said quickly. "That was rude of me. But—"

Kate Madison held up a warning hand. "You'd better stop there or you'll spoil what began as a handsome apology. We'll call a truce for the time being, and I'll have another talk with you later. That's if I think there's any point in it. Now here comes Eyre to find out what I've been saying to you."

Thank heaven for that, Darryn thought, and jumped to her feet so eagerly she was quite sure it would be interpreted in just the way Eyre wanted.

"Finished your talk?" Eyre asked, coming onto the verandah and looking across at Darryn in a way that made her heart thump uncomfortably. He was certainly adept at conveying a passionate reaction to her! "Now I'm through with what I had to see to we can devote ourselves to something really agreeable."

Darryn knew he expected her to walk across to him, but she couldn't do it. Instead, she moved farther away, and hovered at the house door.

"Can we go out and look around a little?" she murmured, and saw a quick shadow of annoyance pass across his face.

"If that's what you want, darling. Go and fetch your hat and we'll get started."

He smiled but she knew he wasn't exactly pleased with her. Still, what did she care? Bother the Madisons, she thought. She didn't intend to spend her time worrying about them. In her room, she hunted around for her white cotton hat and her camera, then stared at her reflection in the mirror. Not a good breeding cow! She giggled aloud at the thought. Would she tell Eyre that? She didn't know whether it would amuse him or not. Anyhow, she was going to get her mind back onto the real reason she was here, which was—

She glanced down at her camera. She wasn't here to take photographs. That was only what she'd told Eyre. She was here to find her Dreaming, her enchanted land. And Eyre was going to think she was out of her mind if she insisted she wanted to visit the stockmen's quarters. With a sigh, she pulled on her hat and picked up her camera, and discovered he was hovering at the verandah door.

"You're taking your time. What's the trouble? Have you lost your enthusiasm?"

Yes, she had. At this moment she didn't care a fig for going out to take photographs, and she tossed her camera down on the bed.

"I'm not ready to take pictures yet. I want to get the

feel of the place. I don't want to rush in and waste a lot of film on nothing," she said perversely.

"Well, that's up to you," he said looking at her through narrowed eyes. "I presume you know what you're talking about. And by the way, that wasn't much of an act you put on just now. If I'm going to spend valuable time escorting you around the property, then you must make a fair return."

Darryn sent him a hostile look and made to walk past him onto the verandah, but he grabbed her arm and jerked her towards him.

"Are you listening?"

She pulled away fiercely. "Yes, I'm listening. You don't have to push me around. What act are you talking about, anyhow? How do I know what you expect me to do—what lies you want me to tell? Were you listening in on that conversation just now?"

"No, I was not," he grated. He strode across the verandah and down the steps, and she had to hurry to keep pace with him along the gravel path. She could smell the oleander flowers, sickly sweet on the hot air, and the subtle scent of gum blossoms from high up in the trees. "I was talking about the way you dived past me on the verandah just now," he said frowning down at her as she panted along at his side. "As though I were someone you hadn't been introduced to."

"Well, I haven't been introduced to you, have I?" she said flippantly. "Did you expect me to rush up and throw my arms around your neck, or something like that?"

"Yes. Something very like that," he said imperturbably. "Try to keep it at the front of your mind for next time, will you? We're madly in love, remember."

Darryn sighed audibly. He opened a gate, and beyond, on a gravel square, a car was drawn up. Eyre opened the door for her and she climbed in. She felt just a little excited at the thought of driving through the big paddocks where her father used to work. It was too bad she had to be in the company of this disturbing man. How, with him around, was she going to be able to tell if there were good vibes for her here? He seemed to come between her and everything with his demands, his forcefulness.

"Have I made my point?" he asked, as he got in behind the wheel and started up the motor.

"Yes, you've made your point," she said limply. "Next time I'm all over you like a rash. I'll remember. . . . Now where are we going? Could we look around the station buildings first?"

"I had something else in mind. You can do that anytime on your own."

His shrug drew her eyes to his broad shoulders. He'd changed into a blue- and white-striped shirt and off-white pants and she supposed he looked attractive. Except that for her taste—good heavens, she thought, a little surprised at herself, was she developing a definite taste in men? That was really something new! Anyhow, for her taste his shoulders were too broad, too muscular. That precluded elegance. Though of course, elegance wasn't something you'd expect of a—a stud bull. She uttered a little spurt of laughter and he asked, "What's funny?"

"Nothing," she said, controlling herself quickly. "I was just thinking of something your grandmother said to me."

She saw his heavy eyebrows go up and he sent her a quick enquiring look. By now, they were following a double red track across a paddock that was a mixture of grey and green and red, with clumps of trees dotted about and gathering into a line farther ahead, along the watercourse. "Well, let's hear about the conversation anyhow. How did it go?"

"Can't you guess? It went like a bomb," Darryn said. "You shouldn't have left me alone with Kate Madison. You must have known she'd get me all boxed up—and tear me to pieces if she could."

"You appear to me to have come out of it alive and kicking, and with more than the usual sparkle in those fiery green eyes of yours," he retorted. "To tell the truth, I rather thought you might charm my grand-mother."

Darryn laughed incredulously. "You must be joking! There wasn't the slightest chance of that. She doesn't like the look of me at all. And I'm quite sure she doesn't think I'm a good breeding cow," she added, widening her eyes and sending him a sidelong glance.

His mouth curved in a wry smile. "Sounds like she's really been talking business. I hope you ignored it." He pointed ahead into the trees. "There's a pretty water hole down there. Does that sort of thing appeal to you photographically? I suppose you're more interested in people, but it could make a beginning. The tranquillity of nature. It could give you a few ideas."

Darryn glanced at him suspiciously. She wasn't all that keen on the tranquillity of nature. Not at this moment, and alone with Eyre. And she rather suspect-ed *he* was the one who was going to get ideas . . .

"I'm not particularly interested in the water hole," she shrugged. "Where is everyone, anyhow? It all looks so empty."

"You're in the outback, Darryn," he said flatly, and kept on driving. "You surely don't expect it to look like a rodeo ground—or King's Cross."

"No, of course I don't," she said impatiently.

"Then why be so hard to get on with? What's wrong with the billabong? I don't want you to have the idea there are no beautiful spots around here."

Darryn's lips tightened. It seemed no use to expect to get her own way where Eyre was concerned. But if he imagined for a moment that they were going to practise love scenes down by the billabong, he was quite wrong.

What on earth had put that idea into her head? she wondered, somewhat taken aback at her thoughts. She leaned back in the seat and looked out into the sunlight, ignoring him.

A few minutes later Eyre pulled up in the shade. He stretched one arm along the seat behind her head and surveyed her clinically.

"What are you up to, Darryn? Making things difficult? Making excuses for pulling out?" Without seeming to move, he reached out and with an indolent gesture flicked the cotton hat off her head.

"What do you mean?" she asked huskily, unnerved by his nearness, by the way he was looking at her, by the knowledge that his thigh was now touching hers and that she was acutely aware of its hardness and its heat; yet refusing to give herself away by shifting along the seat.

"I mean leaving your camera behind, being so hard to please when I'm doing my best to be helpful. There are many sides to outback life, and I understood you wanted to capture as many of them as you could for this editor who's interested in your work."

Darryn turned her head aside. The lie that had seemed so harmless now made her uneasy and she said evasively, "Landscape photography doesn't interest me all that much. I want some human content. And all right, don't say it again," she hurried on. "So the outback's empty. Though at this moment as far as I'm concerned there's just one person too many in it."

"Meaning me," he said, his nostrils widening slightly. He captured a strand of her hair and tugged it not altogether gently. "You're really spoiling for a fight, aren't you? Which brings me back to where we were before: You want to pull out."

"Suppose I do?" she said after a second. Her heart

was beginning to thud and she wished he'd let go of her hair. With a sudden movement she raised her hand and snatched it free, glaring at him angrily.

"Then I'll think you're both ungrateful and without conscience," he said coldly. "What's frightened you off? Something my grandmother said?"

"Maybe," she said defensively. "Also your aunt's attitude. It's not much fun being treated like an unwanted guest."

"Has Ruth made you feel like that? I'm sure Kate hasn't, nor I. Nor Andrew. Come on now, Darryn, you know we're all fascinated by you. What more do you want me to say?"

His eyes moved over her slowly, assessingly, and she could feel the quickening of her pulse rate, the rise and fall of her breast. She simply didn't know how to take his remarks, and with a swift movement she opened the car door and slithered out.

"I suppose I might as well take a look at your damned water hole," she said.

A few seconds later, she wished she'd brought her camera with her after all. The water hole was unexpectedly beautiful. Trees crowded thickly around it, the reflections in the water were brilliant, and the unbelievably red sand was pitted here and there with the tiny tracks of animals.

Darryn squatted down on her heels by the water while Eyre stood silently behind her. Soon she forgot he was there, as she mindlessly enjoyed all that nature had to offer: the aromatic scent of leaves, the glitter of the water as its mirrored pictures moved in the slight breeze, the chatter of parrots as they flew from one tree to another in a game of follow-the-leader.

Eyre was right, this was a wonderful spot to make a beginning before going on to explore Moon Mountain's vast paddocks. Had her father shown her mother this side of the outback? she wondered. She rather thought not. Her mother had stayed moping in the bungalow. And that was a pity.

I could be happy here if I fell in love with a stockman, she thought dreamily . . .

She looked up bemused as Eyre squatted down beside her. Their eyes met and they both smiled faintly, and then Darryn turned quickly away, somehow disturbed.

"The men will be back home tonight," he said after a moment. "They've been mustering the Spring Paddock, branding the calves."

"I thought stockmen always camped out," she said unevenly, still shaken by something that had passed between them when they exchanged that glance.

"Not always. It depends where they're working," he said easily. "The last several days, they've been no more than a few miles out."

They both got to their feet and began to saunter back in the direction of the car.

"Do you remember a stockman called Chris Beresford?" Darryn wanted to ask. She didn't think he would remember. He'd have been in his very early teens when her father worked here, and probably away at boarding school. But whether he remembered or not, he'd be curious if she asked a question like that. And she definitely wasn't going to tell him facts about her life that were very private and very personal.

So there was no point in asking.

They got back into the car in silence.

During the next hour or so, Darryn began to get some idea of how large the station was. When they stopped for a few minutes where cattle had been mustered, she wished she'd brought her camera with her. Instead, she stayed in the car while Eyre strode over to talk to a couple of the stockmen. Her father must have done this kind of work, she thought as she watched a beast being leg-roped, branded, castrated. It was an intimidatingly masculine world, and while she found it exciting, she couldn't imagine her mother fitting into it. No wonder she'd hidden herself away in the bungalow and cried!

"Hi, Darryn." A man had sauntered over to the car to lean down and put his head in at the window. It was Andrew and she snapped out of her reverie and sent him a bright smile.

"Oh, hello Andrew. I didn't see you there."

He wore jeans and a checked shirt, and he looked cheerful though dusty.

"Well, what do you think of it all?—the wide open spaces, the outback?"

"I think it's fabulous," she said after a moment, and he grinned.

"Watch it! The thrill will soon wear off, and then boredom will set in."

"Are *you* bored?" she challenged.

"I'm here to learn management. Once I'm through with that, you won't catch me staying in the outback. I'm heading for somewhere more civilised, preferably not too far from Brisbane. I want to get married, and I reckon I'll have a better chance of persuading some nice girl to take me on in Queensland."

Darryn widened her eyes. "I wouldn't mind living here. I couldn't care less about being close to the city."

Andrew raised one eyebrow. "You really are keen on the Boss, aren't you? I'd advise you to hold your horses. To put it bluntly, you're not the only girl in the picture."

"Do you mean Cyrilla?" she asked quickly, and he nodded. "I know about her—that she's coming here on a visit. But as it happens, I'm not—" She stopped abruptly, on the point of admitting that she wasn't in love with Eyre.

"You aren't worried," he finished for her. "Well, I haven't met the other lady, but I wish you luck. . . . I'd better get back to work. Here comes the Boss." He sauntered off, nodding to Eyre as they passed each other.

"Fascinating the jackeroo again?" Eyre asked as he climbed in behind the wheel.

"I didn't whistle him up," Darryn retorted. "He came to speak to me just out of friendliness."

"And how friendly were *you?*" he demanded as they started off in a cloud of red dust.

"Well?" He turned his head and frowned at her when she didn't answer, and she said slowly, "I don't understand you, Mr.—Eyre. You talk as if—"

"As if I were serious? I am serious. You're not going to treat this as a game."

"I thought it was a game," she said mildly.

"As far as you and I are concerned, yes. But we're the only two players. Remember that."

"Don't worry. I'm not setting out to fascinate Andrew. We were only talking. He was telling me that when he's finished his training here, he intends to leave the outback and work somewhere not so isolated."

"Giving himself a better chance to find a wife? Oh, I know. Well, this is not his territory. I was born and bred here."

"How does Cyrilla feel about the outback?" Darryn asked after a moment.

"Why bring Cyrilla into it?" he asked dryly. "I've told you I'm not interested in my family's plans for me and Cyrilla. I daresay she'd fit into the life here if she wanted to. And if she were asked. But I don't intend asking her."

"Then who—" Darryn began. She started again. "Your grandmother wants to see you settled. She's worried about what you do with your life."

"Kate's not a worrier," he said dismissively. "She always makes the best of things."

Did she? Then in that case, why didn't he tell her he

meant to marry Ellen Dwyer? But of course there was something distasteful in the notion that two people were waiting for a third to die so that they could marry. Not liking her thoughts, she put them aside abruptly and devoted herself to asking Eyre questions about the cattle station.

Back at the homestead, Darryn went straight to her room. She decided that she was going to dress up just a little for dinner. For the honour of the family. The *Beresford* family.

She knew when she emerged from the bathroom where she'd showered that the stockmen were back in their quarters. She could hear voices in the distance, and from the long windows in her room she could see lights among the trees. She hadn't finished her unpacking, but she dressed quickly, choosing a black dress that was rather formal but very simple. Her only ornament was a dark green metallic rose, rather flattened from being packed away in her suitcase, and generally worn at the low V-neck of her dress. Tonight she clipped it in her vibrantly bright hair, where it glowed in somber contrast.

Dressed, her light make-up quickly applied, she went onto the verandah. A huge warmly golden moon had risen above the trees to wash the garden with its hot light, and she crossed the verandah restlessly and went into the garden, following a path that took her past the house, through a white gate that opened onto a grove of orange trees. Beyond was a hedge of oleanders, and another gravel path shadowed by tall trees that stood motionless in the warm moonlit night. A little awkward in her thin-soled, high-heeled sandals, she wandered on, leaving the lights of the homestead behind her.

Presently she found herself approaching some bungalows and a long verandahed building. Warm yellow lights streamed out across a courtyard shaded by big spreading trees. The stockmen's quarters, she thought with a faint shock, and stood staring, aware now of voices, faint music. This was where her father had lived.

A man came onto the verandah and stood silhouetted against the light from an open doorway. Darryn kept perfectly still. She knew he was staring at her, and she had a mad desire to speak to him. But what could she say? She stared at the broad-shouldered faceless stockman for a long moment, then turned helplessly, and hurried back towards the homestead.

In the orange orchard, beyond the oleander hedge, she paused to regain her breath. She thought of her mother who'd come to one of those cottages when she'd married—and had never been asked to the homestead. *If I'd been born here—brought up here*, Darryn thought, *that would be where I belonged*. Instead, ironically, she was the Madisons' guest.

"Is that you, Darryn? I've been looking for you all over the place. Are you coming in to have a drink before dinner?"

It was Eyre, and Darryn forced a bright smile.

"Yes, of course. I was just taking a stroll in the moonlight." She sounded breathless and oddly guilty, and that was how she felt, and she tensed when Eyre took her arm.

"And what happened?"

"N-nothing. What do you mean? I saw one of the stockmen, that's all."

"Is it? Then how come you're standing here gasping like a fish and trembling when I touch you?"

"I'm not," she denied, pulling away from him quickly. "I've been hurrying. I thought I might be late for dinner—"

To her relief he didn't press the point, but he took hold of her arm again.

"It's time you started acting like a girl in love."

Darryn sighed exasperatedly as they began to walk through the orange trees together.

"It's easy to talk, but I don't know that I can," she muttered.

"Why not? Haven't you ever been in love?"

"Not really," she said unwillingly. "Besides, we hardly know each other." She wanted to snatch her hand away from him again, because now he wasn't holding her arm; his fingers had slid down to her wrist, and his thumb was stroking the silky skin there with a soft circular movement. Maybe he was taking her pulse, she thought wildly, and instantly felt it quicken alarmingly.

They'd reached the gate that led out of the orange orchard, but instead of opening it and letting her through he took hold of her other hand and drew her against him. She felt his mouth on her forehead, the heat of his breath.

"Maybe you need warming up before you can perform," he murmured, his arms closing around her slim form as he pulled her more closely against him.

Darryn struggled slightly, too much aware of the muscularity of his thighs pressed so firmly against her own, and of the pounding of her heart. She raised her face and could see the gleam of his eyes as he looked down at her compellingly.

"We don't have to do this," she said huskily. "Just—just tell me how you want me to behave, and I'll do my best."

He shook his head firmly. "A little practical experience is what you need, Darryn," he murmured, his mouth curving in a quizzical smile. One hard finger touched her lips, then his hand caressed her cheek before sliding down to her throat and lying against the bare skin in the deep V of her neckline. She stiffened as his fingers pushed aside the soft material of her dress, and stroked the swell of her breast tentatively. If he dared go any further than this she was going to scream. She'd promised herself that if he went too far, she'd disappear, and so she would.

She drew a deep breath as his exploratory hand moved on, tracing the shape of her breast through the stuff of her dress—and no doubt feeling the racing of her heart before coming to rest on her rib cage. His head bent to hers and his mouth found her own, and Darryn felt herself go limp.

She wanted him to kiss her now. The feel of his mouth reminded her of the night he'd kissed her in Alice Springs, of the pleasure she'd felt then—

His lips moved over hers sensuously, softly, as if they were searching for something. His lower lip met hers, then his tongue touched her upper lip tantalisingly and suddenly all her awareness was concentrated on the reactions he was invoking. She felt her lips grow warm and soft, and when he began kissing her she opened her mouth to him, feeling pleasure spread like a gentle flame along every nerve in her body.

She could hardly breathe when he let her go. She felt drugged, dazed, and she leaned her cheek against his chest and closed her eyes.

When she opened them, she saw that Ruth Nash had come onto the verandah, and she understood exactly why Eyre had played out that little scene.

"That should give my aunt a pretty fair idea of how we feel about each other," he murmured as, his arm about her, they went into the house together.

Chapter Five

Darryn noticed a decided chill in Ruth's manner towards her that night, not only at dinner but also afterwards, in the sitting room. Kate had gone to bed, and Eyre disappeared with Andrew to the men's quarters.

"Don't go to bed yet, darling," he told Darryn, turning back for a moment as he reached the door. "We can have an hour or so together when I come back."

She murmured something unintelligible and felt the colour flood her cheeks. It was particularly infuriating because she didn't normally blush, yet lately it seemed to be happening to her more and more.

When Eyre had gone, there was silence in the room. Ruth took up some needlework, and Darryn asked brightly, "What are you making, Mrs. Nash?"

"I'm embroidering a piano stool cover for one of my nieces in Adelaide. Catherine, Eyre's sister. I don't suppose you've met her."

"Not yet." Darryn stood up restlessly and moved across to the radio. "Do you mind if I play some music?"

"Well, I have a slight headache, but if you can't find any other way of amusing yourself and don't want to talk—" Ruth paused, looking at Darryn over the glasses she evidently needed for close work.

Darryn sat down again defeated. She definitely didn't want to talk, but she had little choice. What a mess she was getting into! She almost wished she could simply walk out on it all—go back to Alice Springs. *Almost.*

She'd slumped back in her chair and was twisting her fingers together nervously when she found Ruth Nash was looking at her piercingly. She searched rapidly in her mind for something safe to talk about, and came up with photography. With the hope that she might speak of her interest as an eager amateur, she framed an opening remark only to have Ruth speak first.

"I'd like you to tell me something about yourself, Darryn. It's nice to know a little about one's guests, especially in an isolated place like this."

Darryn swallowed. Those icy eyes were making her uncomfortable, and the only possible thing to do seemed to be to rush in and put into words what Eyre had asked her to act out. Then perhaps Ruth would be convinced, and Darryn would be able to go back to Alice Springs, there to come to terms with whatever personal discoveries she'd made at Moon Mountain.

"I suppose the main thing you want to know about is my relationship with Eyre," she said, sitting up straight and widening her green eyes at Ruth who looked somewhat taken aback at the baldness of her statement.

"Oh, I wouldn't dream of asking impertinent questions, Darryn," Ruth murmured.

"It's quite all right, Mrs. Nash." Darryn smiled determinedly. "There's nothing to hide. Eyre and I are—very much in love." She fiddled with the flower in her hair, and Ruth stared at her with open hostility.

"Dear me," she said at last, with a little laugh. "You're so very young, aren't you?"

Young? What on earth had that to do with it? "I'm twenty," Darryn said flushing. "Kate—Mrs. Madison —was telling me she was only eighteen when she married and came to Moon Mountain."

"Ah, but she was a country girl," Ruth said as if that were significant. "But you're not trying to tell me that Eyre has actually asked you to marry him, are you?"

Darryn couldn't say yes. Nor could she say that he hadn't, and he wasn't going to, and that even if he did, she'd refuse. She'd pulled the flower out of her hair and her fingers were occupied in smoothing the stiff bronze-green petals.

"Not exactly." She raised her lashes and looked at Ruth. "But he isn't going to marry Cyrilla, you know. Oh, I know everyone wants him to marry so Mrs. Madison can go and live with you in Adelaide. Eyre's told me all about that. But he's still not going to marry Cyrilla, and it's really silly for you to make plans and think you can—manipulate him."

Ruth's face reddened. "I'm not going to argue about that, Darryn. You've told me all I need to know. I hardly thought Eyre would have already asked you to marry him since it's obvious you must scarcely know each other, and I'm quite sure he won't. He does some rash things, but he doesn't see marriage as a game. You're very pretty, very charming, but Eyre will soon come down to earth. I'm sure he's enjoying your company just now, but I know how he feels about Cyrilla, though obviously you don't."

"But I do know," Darryn contradicted her. Eyre had no more intention of marrying Cyrilla than he had of marrying her, but it was not for her to explain the reason for that. "You're quite wrong, Mrs. Nash. Why don't you leave him alone?"

The older woman carefully gathered up her needle-work and got to her feet. She looked down at Darryn haughtily. "I've told you I'm not going to argue with you, Darryn. Please excuse me. I'm going to bed. Play some records if you want to—my bedroom's on the other side of the house. Good night. Don't keep Eyre up too late, will you?"

She left the room, and Darryn expelled her breath and grimaced. Playing this role was not exactly a lot of fun! *I should be paid for doing it,* she thought ruefully, and she was only half joking.

She no longer felt like listening to music, and she wasn't going to wait about for Eyre either. She'd had about all she could stand of the Madisons for one day, in fact, and after a moment's thought, she went to her room, got into bed as fast as she could, and switched off the light.

She slept like a log.

She heard the clatter of the stockmen and their horses at some unearthly hour in the morning when it was scarcely light, and she lay between sleep and waking thinking of her parents. How had her mother felt in the early mornings when Chris Beresford left her to go out on the run? Had she lain in bed and cried and wished she'd never married him? Or had she, for just a while anyhow, been so madly in love with him that she simply lay dreaming about him? And longed all day for him to come back home to her . . .

I would, Darryn thought drowsily, and was shocked wide awake by the discovery that the face she was conjuring up in her mind was Eyre Madison's face.

Well, she wasn't going to lie in bed thinking of him. He'd probably gone out with the stockmen this morning, and she hoped he had. Perhaps if she'd waited for him last night, he might have asked her to come out too. But right now she was going to get up and prowl about on her own and do some thinking. She didn't

have to stay around here playing at being in love with
him every second of the day—particularly not at this
early hour, when the womenfolk would still be in bed.

In five minutes she was up and dressed, in jeans, shirt
and sneakers. Her shining hair was caught back at her
nape with a narrow black ribbon, her face bare of
make-up, and she felt good as she tiptoed across the
verandah towards a world that still looked shadowy and
unreal.

She'd got as far as the oleander hedge when Eyre
caught up with her, and she stopped in her tracks, her
heart pounding furiously. Bother him—spoiling her
fun! She had a nasty feeling there was trouble in store
for her, because she hadn't obeyed orders last night.
Perhaps he'd be mollified when she told him how she'd
tackled his aunt!

"What are you doing up and about so early in the
morning?" he asked as she turned to acknowledge his
greeting. His aquamarine eyes angled over her trim
figure before returning to her face. "Where's your
camera?"

"I'm just reconnoitering at the moment," she said
defensively. "That's why I'm up so bright and early. I
want to see things for myself in my own way."

They stood by the oleanders where the warm musky
scent of the flowers hung on the air. The sun had barely
risen, the world was cool and beautiful, the sky still
pearly as fleeting clouds drifted away from the sun haze
low on the horizon. A flock of galahs flew down to
some hidden pool in the river bed, their pink breasts
glowing, their cries raucous and cheeky.

"For yourself? Or by yourself?" Eyre was looking
down at her narrowly. "Are you telling me you don't
want my company? You don't believe in flattery, do
you? I'd like to hear why you disappeared to bed so
early last night and didn't wait up for me, by the way."

Darryn shrugged. "I was tired. Besides, there was no

point. She—your aunt—had gone to bed. There was no one around to impress."

"Nevertheless, believe it or not, I wanted to talk to you," he said raising his eyebrows.

"What about?" she asked uneasily. For some reason she thought of what Margo had said—"He's susceptible —anything could happen—"

"About you, of course. I want to find out what makes you tick."

"Why should you care? Besides, I don't tick," she exclaimed, disconcerted, and then bit her lip, aware of how senseless that must have sounded—and was.

"Oh, you tick all right, Darryn," he said, running his fingers through his thick brown hair. "Right now, you're ticking away like a time bomb."

"Ready to explode, you mean? Well, I had your aunt ticking like a time bomb last night. I told her—" She stopped, discovering she didn't like admitting she'd told his aunt they were in love, and that she'd also implied he intended marrying her.

"Well, go on—what did you tell her?" Eyre insisted when she was silent.

She shrugged. "More or less what you told me to," she said shortly.

"That we're madly in love?" he said mockingly.

"Words to that effect," she said, embarrassed, and began to walk ahead of him through the trees. "I said you weren't going to marry Cyrilla, and she wasn't a bit pleased. But I know she didn't believe me, though she was very polite about it."

"Ruth is usually polite," he agreed. "What did she say?"

"That'd you'd come down to earth when Cyrilla turned up," she said over her shoulder. "Will you?" she added, pretending ignorance of his affair with Ellen Dwyer.

"No, I won't," he said shortly. "I wouldn't have

brought you here if that were the case. Surely you know that."

"Oh, *I* may know," Darryn agreed. "But your aunt doesn't. Cyrilla's still coming," she reminded him. "And no matter what you say, I'm not looking forward to *that*. I'm going to hate it."

"I'll see if we can't remedy that somehow," he said lightly. He'd caught up with her and, flinging an arm carelessly around her shoulders, he pulled her against him briefly. Darryn stiffened momentarily, but let his arm stay where it was. She could feel the warmth of his skin against her neck, the heaviness of his muscled arm as it imprisoned her. She had a sudden crazy impulse to tell him about her parents, to reveal that he and she might have met years ago if her mother hadn't run away from the outback. Imagine it! They could have known each other well! But not all that well, she reminded herself realistically. It was unlikely Eyre Madison would have had much to do with the daughter of one of his stockmen.

She glanced up at him and caught his eye and looked quickly away again. She wasn't going to confide in him of course. It would only make the situation between them even harder to put up with.

He removed his arm and flipped the hair back from her neck.

"Your hair amazes me. I hope to heaven that's its natural colour."

Why on earth should he care? she wondered, a little shaken by some unfamiliar note in his voice. It seemed a—funny sort of thing for him to say. Did he mean he *liked* red hair? Or that it wasn't the sort of colour a normal person would actually choose?

"I was born with it," she said. They'd nearly reached the stockmen's quarters now, but instead of continuing on the way she'd walked last night, they turned off along a path that led towards the big trees that marked the course of the river. "My mother has hair exactly the same colour. Still. And she's forty."

"Only forty? You marry young in your family, do you? Have you any brothers and sisters?"

"No. I'm an only child."

"And a spoiled one?"

She flashed him a glance. If that was what he thought, he was very wrong, but she said moderately, "I don't think so. My parents are more wrapped up in their work than in me. They're not all that mad about having children. If they were, they might have—"

She broke off to look at one of the big River Red gums that edged the river bed that was now visible. Gnarled and twisted, its mighty branches were flung out in almost histrionic gestures, and its massive white trunk was patterned with splashes of red and grey and mauve. In the white sand of the river bed sprawled a huge sheet of pale green water. The fleeting pink light from the sky shimmered over its faintly rippled surface, and towards the farther bank, its depths were shadowed by craggy red rocks, from which sprang the immaculate white trunks of graceful ghost gums.

"Is it safe to swim here?" she asked Eyre, who had stood silently at her side while she looked her fill.

"Sure. The water's been cleared of snags since the bed last flooded. But to resume our conversation, what is it your parents do that keeps them from doting on you, Darryn? Or from wanting a bigger family?"

"They both lecture at the university."

"Academics? I'd never have guessed it. You don't take after them, then?"

"Does it look like it? I'm not even wild about living in the city. Half my life, all I've wanted was to come outback. It's where I—" She stopped, a little shocked that she'd been on the brink of confession, then finished hastily, "You see, I do have—relatives in the country. My father, as a matter of fact—my real father, that is."

"He's dead?"

"My mother's divorced," she said, avoiding a direct answer. It was strange, but it had never occurred to her that her father could be dead. After all, he'd still be young—not much over forty. Not all that much older than Eyre Madison.

"I'm beginning to work you out just a little," Eyre commented. "You're self-sufficient because you've had to be. You're not necessary to your parents' happiness. Am I right?"

"I'm not given to introspection," she said, blinking slightly. He was right, she supposed, but it was something she'd never dwelt on. The fact that her mother would so much sooner not have had any children . . .

Presently they made their way back to the house for breakfast. The sun was well and truly up now. All the soft hazy colours had given way to brilliance, and the air in the garden was full of warm flower scents. A man was working in the yard; in the homestead, though Kate was still in bed, Ruth was up and about and Andrew had presumably left long since with the stockmen. And judging from the delicious aromas that floated round the verandah, breakfast was ready.

Darryn lost no time in joining Ruth and Eyre at breakfast which was set out on a big table at the end of one of the verandahs. She was ready to eat with appetite a good helping of steak and eggs and toast, followed by tea from the big pot that stood at one end of the table.

This morning, Ruth's politeness extended only as far as inquiring if Darryn had slept well, and then she went on to talk of the party she and Kate were planning.

"I thought perhaps it might be nice to see if Gillian or

Catherine would like to come up from Adelaide with Cyrilla, Eyre," she remarked. "What do you think?"

"You and Kate can please yourselves about that," Eyre said indifferently. "Frankly, I can't see either of my sisters rushing it. It's a damned long way to come for nothing in particular. Though Kate would probably enjoy seeing them. Just what's all the socialising in aid of?" he added casually, reaching for the orange jam. "To give Cyrilla a good time?"

Ruth set down her knife and fork and sent Darryn a swift and unfriendly glance. "It could be the last party mother will attend on Moon Mountain before she settles down in Adelaide, Eyre."

"I hardly think so," Eyre said with a shrug. "If she means to sit tight until my wedding, then she's sure to want a party to celebrate the—er—engagement." Ignoring the look of exasperation that crossed Ruth's face, he went on smoothly, "You can count me out this time, at all events. I'm more likely to be out at the muster camp than here when your wassailing is under way."

Ruth frowned. "At the muster camp? But surely you can't mean to camp out. You really must be here. I've asked a number of people to come, and besides, there's Cyrilla—she'll be so hurt—"

"Cyrilla's not my guest," he said bluntly, and Darryn cringed inwardly. "We'll be mustering the Mountain Paddock shortly, and while I'm prepared to give Andy all the responsibility I think he can handle, I mean to be out there myself for at least part of the time."

"But why?" Ruth persisted. "I thought you always mustered the Mountain Paddock from the air nowadays. It's not as if Andrew will be on his own. Chris will be there. He's experienced—he'll see that everything goes as it should."

Eyre was draining his cup, and Darryn, whose ears

had pricked up at the mention of the name Chris, asked quickly, "Who's Chris?"

Both Ruth and Eyre looked at her in surprise and she flushed with embarrassment.

"My head stockman," Eyre said unhelpfully as he set his cup down. He proceeded to tell Ruth, "That paddock's too important for me to place the onus of it on somebody else, however competent. The cattle out there have been getting very cunning over the past couple of years. They're so used to the plane they've taken to hiding amongst the trees. That's why we're using horses again. I don't want a lot of scrub bulls running around loose and ruining the quality of my beef. So just don't expect me to shelve my work to attend a party, Ruth." He pushed his chair back as he spoke and told Darryn, "I'm working today, Darryn. You'll have to amuse yourself. Take a swim—go for a drive. But don't get lost. Right?"

"I don't drive," Darryn said, resentful to learn that he was going out and leaving her to her own devices. "I do ride, though, so maybe I could have one of the horses."

"Sorry," he said, his voice hard. "I think not. When I have time I'll take you out riding myself."

"Can't I come with you today?" she said quickly. "I wouldn't be a nuisance."

"I'm afraid you would be," he said flatly, and strode towards the door into the house.

Chagrined, furious with him for treating her like that—when he was meant to be mad about her— Darryn ran after him and seized his arm.

"Why can't I go with you? Where are you going? Out to wherever the stockmen are? I want to go—"

"Look—just don't make a nuisance of yourself, Darryn," he said lowering his voice and drawing her into the hallway where Ruth couldn't hear them.

"A nuisance! Is that what you call it?" she exclaimed.

"I thought we were to impress on your aunt how mad we are about each other. Or do you want it to look as though *I'm* chasing *you* now? Because I assure you, I'm not."

"Aren't you?" He raised his eyebrows and pried her fingers from his arm. "It looks very much like it at the moment. At all events, I can't waste my time on you today and that's flat."

"So what am I supposed to do?" she demanded. "Waste *my* time hovering around the house all day?"

"What's wrong with taking a few pictures?" he said unsympathetically. "It's all part of outback life, you know—the women left behind in the homestead while the men are out with the cattle. And you'd better resign yourself to the fact that you'll probably have to do your own thing for a couple more days after this."

"Well that's great," Darryn said bitterly. He'd said nothing about this earlier on, he'd left her completely in the dark, and she didn't like being treated so casually. Not when she was doing him a favour. "The dice certainly seem to be loaded in your favour, don't they?"

"I gathered from what you said this morning that you're more or less where you want to be—in the outback," he reminded her sardonically. "You haven't really got much to complain about. I haven't taken your camera away from you, and you've already let me know you don't care much for my company. So cheer up."

Darryn could have screamed. "And when you're camping out at the Mountain Paddock—will I be left behind with Cyrilla to cope with all the havoc you seem to leave trailing behind you?"

"I'll think about it," he said maddeningly. "I'll see you tonight, Darryn."

"I can hardly wait," Darryn said coldly.

He looked at her for a moment. Then unexpectedly he pulled her into his arms and kissed her mouth in a way that made her feel he was doing much more than just that, his body close to hers, his thighs hard and sensual against her own. For a moment she submitted, simply because she was taken by surprise and then with a violent movement she wrenched herself free and smacked his face—hard. Much harder than she meant to, in fact, and she gasped when she saw his eyes blaze and the red colour run into his cheek where her hand had struck it.

"Don't ever do that again," she said, her voice trembling, though more with fear at what she had done than anything else. Her back was pressed to the wall as he stood staring at her, and her legs felt as if they'd give way at any moment. His eyes went to her mouth and she saw a muscle move in his jaw.

"Okay, if that's the way you want it," he said tautly. "But I'd advise you not to lash out at me again, either."

"I will if you provoke me." Her face, that had been pale, began to regain its normal colour. He wasn't going to strike her and he wasn't going to kiss her, and she wasn't sure which she'd been afraid of most. Relaxing slightly, she began to feel glad she'd hit him. She'd promised herself she'd do something like that if he went too far, and he had gone too far.

They stared at each other for a long moment more, then Darryn's eyes fell, and Eyre, with a muttered exclamation she didn't catch, swung away and left her. Her mouth was dry and her legs were like jelly. Worse, she could feel a warmth, a trembling in them where his muscled thighs had impressed themselves.

Well, she was free of him until tonight, she told herself, and drawing a deep breath she tried to pull herself together. What she'd have liked to do was to go to her room and lie on the bed and sleep. But she wasn't going to do that. She was going back to finish her breakfast even if it choked her. Not for anything was she going to let Ruth Nash know that there'd been a scene between herself and Eyre. She wished she hadn't run after him, but it was done now and she had to make the best of it.

Ruth looked at her curiously as she resumed her chair and Darryn helped herself to toast and reached for the teapot, then proceeded to ask bright questions about station work. Ruth was uncooperative, and she soon gave up and began to think about the head stockman, Chris. It couldn't possibly be her father. He'd left Moon Mountain years and years ago, possibly even before she was born. Her mother had told her that when she was petitioning for divorce the lawyers had had a frightful time locating him. Heaven alone knew where he was now . . .

Eyre was away for the next three days, though he came home to sleep. Ruth left Darryn to entertain herself, but on the second afternoon Kate invited her to see her garden of native plants, which Darryn found quite fascinating. Her interest pleased the old lady, who told her the name of each shrub and plant, and Darryn tried to make up her mind which were her favourites—the rich purple flowers of the native fuchsia or the fragile pink blooms of Sturt's Desert Rose. She took a couple of pictures of Kate wearing a straw hat, sturdy boots, a long navy skirt and high-necked pale blue blouse.

Eyre was right, she admitted to herself, it *was* all part of the outback—particularly Kate.

Somewhere along the way, she'd lost her obsession with hunting up the place where her parents had lived together. That was what it seemed to have been now—an obsession. A fixation on a wishful immature dream—to make up for the knowledge that she wasn't really wanted, perhaps.

Meanwhile, Eyre, as far as she knew, was out with his stockmen who were presumably mustering and camping out. Andrew didn't come back to the homestead at night, and when Eyre drove up around sundown, his boots were dusty and he looked tired. All the same, after dinner, he took Darryn for a walk in the garden. She knew quite well it was merely to keep up the pretence that they were in love, and he didn't attempt to kiss her. Darryn found him aloof and difficult, and she had no idea whether it was because she'd slapped his face or for some reason not associated with her. She did her best to make conversation, telling him she'd swum, taken a walk and so on, but in return he told her nothing, which left her feeling helpless and unhappy.

It was only by accident that she discovered where he had been spending his days.

She was coming back to the homestead on the third afternoon after a swim in the pool, thinking restlessly of Eyre and of the unenviable position she was in. The thought of Cyrilla worried her, and it worried her too that Eyre's attitude seemed lately to have altered so drastically. He was no longer supportive when it came to convincing the Madison women that he and Darryn were in love.

Perhaps if he didn't have to go out to the muster tomorrow, Darryn thought, they could get together. He could take her out somewhere to get some pictures for her nonexistent assignment for her nonexistent editor. She didn't seem to know what she wanted any more. Her sentimental journey no longer excited her, and she hoped illogically that her feelings of frustration and disappointment would be dissipated once Eyre was around again.

Instead of returning through the orange orchard, she went round the other side of the house thinking it would be pleasant to take another look at Kate's native garden. As she came through a thick patch of desert Grevilleas, their orange flowers brilliant against the dark narrow leaves, she heard voices and realised that Kate and Ruth were there.

Well, right now she wasn't in the mood for coping with them. Her hair was wet and she wore only her black one-piece swimsuit and beach thongs and somehow she felt all that would put her at a disadvantage. She really shouldn't care what they thought of her, and yet she did, which under the circumstances was just plain stupid.

About to turn back and retrace her steps, she changed her mind when she heard what Kate was saying.

"If poor Harry Dwyer's too ill to run Linette Downs and that wife of his hasn't enough spunk to run it for him, then it's time he put in a manager." There were a few sharp sounds and Darryn guessed Kate was cutting back some dead wood from one of her native shrubs. "I know quite well where Eyre's been working the last three days, though he's kept very quiet about it. I daresay Ellen poured out some tale of woe and disaster in Alice Springs and because of his long-standing friendship with Harry he's gone to the rescue. And that's no way to help them solve their problems. It would be far kinder to force Harry to sort out his affairs before it's too late."

"I can't say I entirely agree with you, Mother," Ruth said, her voice gentler, less dogmatic. "For one thing, I don't believe Harry can be as ill as all that. He's only a little over fifty, surely! He'd find a manager if he really needed one. It's just a matter of time, and if Eyre's willing to help out then why shouldn't he? The overseer must be reliable enough, though I know Ellen complains about him. . . . Between you and me, *I* think Eyre's only too glad of an excuse to get away just now. He knows he's made a silly mistake in bringing that girl home with him."

Oh, does *he?* Darryn thought furiously. She moved

away, guilty at having listened, and hating what she'd heard.

She had several very unpalatable things to digest now, one of them being that Eyre had spent the last few days on the Dwyers' property. Kate and Ruth might think he was helping out a friend, but Darryn knew better. And *she* knew—though Ruth evidently didn't—that Harry Dwyer was, as Kate had suggested and as Margo Talbot had said quite definitely, a very sick man. Eyre wouldn't want the Dwyers to put on a manager, and though he'd undoubtedly need to acquaint himself with the conditions at Linette Downs, Darryn didn't think that was exactly what he'd been doing lately. She knew now why he was so weary, so uninterested in her when he came home at sundown.

Well, she told herself, walking angrily back along the path, as of tonight he could snap out of it. Ruth Nash was going to be shown that she was quite wrong if she thought Eyre regretted bringing Darryn Ross home with him. Moreover, in future she was going to refuse to be left behind when he went out for the day. She didn't intend willingly to give him leave to—to dally with Ellen Dwyer.

Chapter Six

That evening when Eyre drove up to the homestead in the four-wheel drive, Darryn was in her room dressing after a shower. She knew Kate and Ruth were sitting on the verandah catching the evening breeze, and without waiting to slip her bare feet into sandals, she sped round the house and met Eyre as he came up the steps.

She hadn't pinned her hair up and it floated 'round her head, curly and wild and glittery. The red light of the setting sun was flooding the garden, but on this side of the house, the verandah was cool and green from the reflected light of the vines that draped it.

Fully conscious of the two women watching, Darryn ran towards Eyre and flung her arms around his waist in an enveloping hug. She didn't care how cool he'd been towards her lately, or why; she was determined to evoke some response from him now, and to let Ruth Nash see it. If she was no longer quite sure of her motive, it didn't seem to matter. Mainly, she'd told herself as she showered, it was a matter of pride, because she wasn't going to be pushed aside when she'd been inveigled into coming here practically against her will.

She felt the hardness of Eyre's body against her own, smelt his male smell, his sweatiness, felt his muscled back as she wrapped her arms around him and pressed her cheek against his chest. And she felt him stiffen as she'd stiffened in his arms more than once. Well, he'd have to put up with it, that was all.

"I thought you were never coming," she breathed out, loud enough for the Madison ladies to hear. "I've *missed* you, Eyre. You're not going away again tomorrow are you?"

He didn't relax, and she was chillingly conscious that he didn't like the feel of her soft feminine body pressed so closely against him. That was because he'd spent the day with Ellen Dwyer and made love to her, and Darryn hung on to him tighter than ever. *Now who's going to believe you wish you hadn't brought me home!* she thought, gazing up at him through the glitter of her lashes.

He looked back at her unreadably, and then, gripping her wrists hard, he pried her away from him, though he smiled as he did it.

"Okay, that's enough," he muttered, and then added more loudly, "Hold on till I've had a shower, Darryn. I've been out in the sun all day."

"Oh, poor you," she murmured. "Does your head ache? Shall I come and massage your neck? You know how good I am at that."

She linked her arm through his and clung to him as he walked into the house, but once out of sight of the others he shook off her arm roughly.

"What on earth are you playing at, Darryn?"

"What do you think? I'm trying to impress on your family that you're definitely not interested in Cyrilla. Isn't that what you want?"

"Yes, it's what I want, but you're overdoing it," he said, his voice hard. "You don't need to create the impression that you've already gone to bed with me—and are ready to do so again right now."

She blushed scarlet. "They won't think that! Why should they? What have I done?"

"You know what you've done," he said abruptly. "Now shoot off. I don't want you to massage my neck."

"Don't flatter yourself," she flared. "I don't intend to massage your neck. I'll—I'll go and put my shoes on and you can take a shower. You certainly need it. I can't think what you do all day to get yourself into such a mess."

"I suppose it wouldn't occur to you I might be chasing cattle out of the scrub," he said shortly.

"No, it wouldn't," she retorted. "I thought your stockmen were paid to do that for you."

"I've been helping a neighbour," he said, raking his fingers through his hair and pushing her aside.

"Oh—I know all about that," Darryn said after his retreating back. But she didn't say it too loud.

He didn't appear again until dinner time.

He came late to the table, and Darryn deliberately allowed her lip to curl slightly as she glanced across at him in the lamplight. Actually, she was pleased to see him. She'd found it nerve-racking sitting at the table alone with Ruth and Kate. Andrew still wasn't back from the muster, Ruth was decidedly cold towards her, and Kate was beginning to ask questions.

"You're enjoying your visit?" had been her opening gambit, and Darryn had sparkled and smiled and answered enthusiastically.

"Oh—very much. I love it here. I'm hoping Eyre might take me riding tomorrow," she improvised.

"So you ride do you?" asked the old lady, sounding surprised. "Where did you learn? I thought you were a city girl."

"A city girl with a yen for the outback," Darryn said

blithely. "I learned to ride when I went to boarding school in the country one year while my parents were overseas."

"And what does your father do that takes him overseas?" Kate enquired, nodding thoughtfully.

"He's a university lecturer," Darryn said, and wondered whether an academic parent would operate in her favour if she were being considered as a breeding cow.

But that was something she was not to find out just yet, because it was at that moment that Eyre made his appearance, and the subject of Darryn's parents was dropped.

Dinner was nearly over when Ruth said casually, "By the way, Eyre, Cyrilla Goddard is arriving in Alice Springs in two days' time. I suppose it's no use asking if you'll go and meet her. You're too busy."

"Much too busy," he agreed, and Darryn glanced at him swiftly. He was looking strikingly handsome in a cream silk shirt, a dark wine-coloured cravat knotted at his throat, and despite herself a tremor ran along her nerves. "If you will make these arrangements, Ruth, then you must take full responsibility for the consequences." He raised his thick dark lashes as he spoke and looked fully at Darryn, and she felt her heart thud. *She* was one of the consequences, of course.

"If you mean I must meet Cyrilla myself, I'm quite willing," Ruth said. "I'll borrow one of the cars if you can spare it." She turned to Darryn. "You don't drive, do you Darryn?"

Darryn shook her head. She was still feeling unnerved from the way Eyre had been looking at her.

"That's a pity. It's a very useful skill in the outback for a woman. Well, never mind, Cyrilla drives and she can give me a rest on the homeward journey. Perhaps you might like to come along though, while transport's available. There's not very much for you to do here, is there?"

Darryn studied her for a moment, and then looked thoughtfully down at her fruit salad and cream. Was Ruth merely offering her an outing? Or was she implying that it was time she bowed out, moved on? The latter, obviously. While transport's available, she'd said.

No one said anything for a moment. Eyre's mouth had set in a hard line and Darryn had an idea he'd be furious if she said she'd go, and that she wouldn't come back. Yet he'd been so hatefully uncooperative when she'd put on that act this evening. Remembering the way he'd pried her away from him, she still felt resentful. Why should she try to help him out when he was like that? All she was doing was keeping a place warm for Ellen Dwyer, and frankly it didn't appeal to her. So maybe she would leave, and he could see how he liked that!

Meanwhile Ruth—and Eyre—were waiting for her reply, and Kate's bright blue eyes were alive with interest.

"I'll let you know later," she told Ruth with an ingenuous smile, then let her green eyes meet Eyre's enigmatically.

When he took her to walk in the garden that night, she knew he'd bring up the subject of her going to Alice Springs, and the thought of telling him that she'd decided to leave rather appealed to her. But on the other hand, she didn't like the idea of having Ruth triumph over her, which she would do, even if it was very politely. So perhaps her decision would depend on Eyre's attitude. If he rubbed her up the wrong way, he'd better watch out or she'd leave him in the lurch.

Neither of them spoke for some time as they strolled together in the moonlight, walking through the garden, then taking the tree-shadowed path that followed the fence of the home paddock. Ahead, a distant line of low crumpled hills made smoky shadows in the moon mist, and above, drifts of cloud marbled the darkness of the sky.

Glancing up at the man beside her, Darryn felt a shiver go through her. He was a stranger, a man of whom she knew almost nothing. Yet in spite of that, in spite of the fact that she'd known him so short a time and seen so little of him during the past three days, she knew she was drawn to him physically. She remembered uneasily how she'd slapped his face the last time he'd kissed her, and how she'd wound her arms around him this evening, pressing herself against his body. Obviously, *his* mind had been full of Ellen Dwyer. He could hardly tolerate having Darryn Ross even touch him.

His arm brushed against hers and she flinched as a warm wave of feeling suddenly engulfed her. Shockingly, right at this minute she wanted him to take her in his arms, she wanted to lean her head against his chest, to hear the beating of his heart, to feel the warmth of his breath on her hair. To have him raise her face to his and kiss her . . . and if he did, she told herself, breaking up her own reverie, then she was going to hand out the same treatment he'd handed out to her. She wouldn't slap his face this time, she wouldn't dare, but she'd let him know one thing, and that was that she didn't like him touching her.

She quickened her step and moved ahead of him, only to be checked when his arms came around her waist from behind, and he pulled her back.

Instantly, her heart began to pound, and her breath quickened as his hands moved upwards to lie lightly on her breasts.

"Darryn." He spoke softly against the smoothness of

her neck. "You're not letting Ruth talk you into leaving, are you?"

She shook her head dazedly, her eyes half closed, the silver glimmer of the moon dazzling her. It seemed no use to remind herself of the resolution she'd made only a minute ago, she didn't want to move. She was unnervingly conscious of his male body pressed against her back, the hard flat muscles of his stomach, the warmth of his thighs where they touched her buttocks. One hand had slid down to rest on her stomach, the other brushed sensuously and tantalisingly across the tips of her breasts, and she closed her eyes and relaxed against him, her whole body unbearably stirred. In a moment she was going to turn to him—she wouldn't be able to help herself . . . to put her arms around his neck and pull his mouth down to hers.

And if she did that, she must be clean out of her mind.

She shivered, though the night air was warm on her bare shoulders and her cheeks were hot, and with an abrupt movement she freed herself from him.

"Let's go back to the house," she said, her voice shaking.

"Not yet," he said, and weakly, instead of insisting, she moved away to lean her trembling body against the powdery trunk of a ghost gum.

He took cigarettes from his pocket and lit one, offering it to her then putting it back between his own lips when she shook her head.

"I didn't know you smoked," she murmured.

"I don't as a rule. Do I gather you don't approve?"

"I don't care what you do," she said coolly. He was standing close to her, and she looked away from him. The ghost gums gleamed around her, their trunks smooth and pale, like the bodies of naked girls, while at her feet the spiky grass was dappled with moonlight and shadow. "Does—," she began, then bit her lip. Does Ellen Dwyer mind if you smoke? she'd been going to ask, but that was none of her business of course.

"Does what?" he prompted.

"Does it matter?" she improvised swiftly. "And suppose I do decide to go to Alice Springs and stay there, does *that* matter?"

"To me?" he said after a moment. "What do you want me to say, Darryn?"

Something in the tone of his voice made her heart shake, and she reminded herself furiously that Margo had told her not to let this virile man get under her skin. That was exactly what she was doing—falling as fast as ever she could for his—his sexual gambits.

She leaned back against the tree and told herself sternly to keep her head. Yet when he stretched out his hand and stroked her bare shoulder a shiver of delight ran instantly along her nerves. His cigarette was a tiny red glowing spot in a world that otherwise was almost devoid of colour, and her eyes strayed to the dark hair that showed in the open V of his shirt, for he'd discarded the cravat he'd worn at the dinner table. The planes of his face were emphasised by the moonlight, and she was deeply aware of the power of his very masculine aura.

"What, Darryn?" he repeated, his fingers still on her bare skin.

With an effort, she brought her mind back to their sporadic conversation.

"I don't want you to say anything in particular," she said huskily. "I just meant I'm sure you can cope with Cyrilla Goddard without my help. Anyhow, I've—had enough."

"Enough of what?" He tossed down his partially smoked cigarette and ground it out carefully with his heel, then put his hands on his narrow hips as his eyes looked penetratingly into hers. "Of the outback? I thought you'd decided you had some affinity with it, that you were all excited about making a photographic record of the life here. Wasn't that why you came?"

"Yes. But you haven't made it possible for me to see much, have you? And I don't like being made a fool of," she said looking straight at him.

"For God's sake—I've been busy. You know that. And who's making a fool of you, Darryn?"

"You are. Who would you think?" she exclaimed. On the point of telling him she knew all about Ellen Dwyer, she realised he might choose to interpret that as jealousy. And she was definitely not jealous. She might find him physically attractive, but that was all. She hurried on, "You tell me to act as if we're madly in love and then you leave me flat. What am I supposed to do to convince everyone? Go around kissing your photo or your boots or something?"

"Well, I'd far sooner you kissed me," he said with a low laugh, and she drew a sharp breath. When he moved towards her she flung out her arms wildly and side-stepped him, nearly losing her balance in the process.

"I'm not interested in your kisses, Mr. Madison," she breathed. "You know very well that's not what I came to Moon Mountain for. It seems to be quite pointless staying. I—I'm going to leave with your aunt. Now you know, and you can do what you like about it," she concluded shakily.

On the brink of sudden tears, she began to run back along the path. She fully expected him to come after her, to smooth her down, to exercise his charm on her, even to try to persuade her to stay. But he didn't, and to her fury she went all the way back to the house alone.

She slept badly that night and got up late. Everyone had breakfasted, and apparently no one was bothered about her nonappearance, which did nothing for her low spirits. For once, she wasn't even hungry, but when Essie, one of the house girls, brought a plate of eggs and bacon, obviously cooked especially for her, to the breakfast room, she forced herself to eat. She saw nothing of Eyre. He must have gone out to Dwyers' again, she thought, depressed. Well, what if he had? Why should she care?

So she didn't care. But surely on her last day he could have put himself out to see she got at least a taste of what she'd come here for.

As she went along the verandah after breakfast, she saw Ruth in the garden, and wondered fleetingly if she should ask her where Eyre was. But that would only invite a politely veiled reminder that Eyre had lost whatever interest he had had in her. The homestead was empty of everyone but the house girls, and Darryn wandered about disconsolately, ashamed of the way she'd behaved last night, blaming Eyre for it, and hating him. She wished that tomorrow would come so that she could be done with Moon Mountain and everyone who belonged there.

She was in her room folding away some of her clothes when Ruth, her arms full of flowers, came to the door. "Oh, you're up, Darryn. Eyre's in the garden talking to Mother, if you were looking for him. I wouldn't interrupt them if I were you. They're probably discussing station affairs. Have you decided whether you're coming to Alice Springs with me tomorrow?"

Darryn had, but she said perversely, just as if she didn't know what Ruth meant, "I don't know. I'm not all that keen on such a long drive for nothing, Mrs. Nash."

"It could be the best thing to do, Darryn," the older woman said after a moment. "Don't you think so?"

Darryn looked at her. There was no malice at all in her face and she thought ruefully, *She really means it. She really believes Eyre will settle for Cyrilla. But he won't.* She felt impatient with Eyre. Why couldn't he have come into the open about his intentions and so have saved all this bother? Though for all she knew, right at this minute he could be explaining himself to Kate. Particularly since she, Darryn, his supposed protector, was leaving in the morning. She'd be well out of it, she decided.

"Think about it, Darryn," Ruth said. "You're a nice girl, and Eyre's behaving very badly. You'll be happier away from here." With a pleasant smile, she drifted off.

Darryn sank down on the side of the bed and caught sight of her face in the mirror. She looked completely miserable and that was how she felt. She'd wanted Eyre to persuade her to stay, yet even if he had, it wouldn't really have changed anything. Not anything that mattered. And she wasn't going to examine *that* thought.

With sudden decision she jumped to her feet, picked up her camera and went outside. She was going to take photographs of everything within sight. At least she'd have something to pore over when she was back in Alice Springs. Later she could go out to some of the cattle stations around Alice and take pictures of the stockmen. Oh yes, life would go on.

She came in late to lunch, her face flushed from the sun and from her long walk. She'd taken pictures of the horses in the paddock and of the yardman; of the old aboriginal who tended the vegetable garden; of the stockman's wife hanging out her washing on the line under the gum trees. And she had several photos, which she knew were going to be terrific, of two small aboriginal children playing with their dog in the red sand on the river bank some half a mile away.

She apologised to everyone for being late, and Eyre drew out a chair for her without comment. Darryn thanked him, but didn't meet his eyes.

Presently, Kate asked Darryn what she'd been doing with herself all morning.

"I expected you to come and see me in amongst my wildflowers. What have you been up to that's put such colour in your cheeks?"

"I've been for a walk," Darryn said, helping herself to cold meat and salad and reflecting that at least she had her appetite back. "I took a few photos along the way. They'll be—tender souvenirs," she added and noted Eyre's look of displeasure at her sardonic tone. Ruth glanced at her thoughtfully, or perhaps it was hopefully, and Kate put her silvery head on one side, her sapphire eyes bright.

"Souvenirs already? When are you leaving us? Not too soon, I hope. Ruth's planning a party, you know. Eyre, pass me the bread."

Eyre obliged, remarking as he did so, "Darryn and I have yet to discuss her departure, Kate."

"Oh indeed! Then don't let me interfere. The girl says she rides, so why don't you take her out this afternoon? Then you can discuss it to your heart's content," the old lady said.

Not surprisingly, Eyre didn't respond. He changed the subject and began to talk about the big muster out at the Mountain Paddock and what he hoped from it. How many head of cattle would be brought in, how many beasts they could expect to cut out for sale, and what condition they'd be in.

"We'll sell them as stores. We always have from out there," Kate said decidedly. "You surely don't have ideas of fattening them up on the Barkly, Eyre!"

It was all talk designed to exclude her, Darryn thought. She caught Ruth looking at her with a gleam of sympathy in her eye which seemed to say, "Isn't it plain that Eyre's not really interested in you?" It was, but it would be a shock to Ruth to discover why.

Darryn turned her head away and tried to decide what she'd do during the afternoon. Wander off by herself and take some more photographs, probably.

Unless Eyre did mean to talk to her about her departure. She didn't think he would try to persuade her to stay at Moon Mountain any longer, but if he did, she had a fair idea of the kind of tactics he'd use, and she was going to be well and truly on her guard. She wasn't going to let him come within kissing distance of her. Ruth was right. Darryn Ross would be happier away from Moon Mountain and the Madisons.

"To return to my suggestion, Eyre," Kate said just before they left the table. "Which horse shall we let Darryn ride? It might be best for her to take Pompon. She was never afflicted by nerves though she has plenty of spirit. What do you think, Darryn? Are you a confident rider or a timid one?"

Darryn bit her lip. She hadn't ridden for ages, and the old lady probably knew it.

"Eyre doesn't have to take me riding, Mrs. Madison. I can amuse myself this afternoon. I don't want to be a nuisance," she added giving Eyre a scathing look.

"A nuisance? What a thing to say!" Kate exclaimed. "Why should you be a nuisance? Eyre invited you here, and he's been too busy to entertain you so far. Of course he's going to take you out riding."

Of course he's not, Darryn thought. If she knew the least little thing about Eyre, the best way to stop him from doing a thing was to try to insist that he should do it. And who knew, perhaps that was Kate's idea.

If it was, it didn't work. To her surprise, Eyre had Pompon saddled for her, and he took her riding.

She didn't enjoy herself very much, though she acquitted herself fairly creditably on Pompon, a little jet black mare that was far from being insultingly docile. Eyre was so polite and impersonal, it made her freeze up inside. In spite of everything she was desperately aware of him, but it seemed that Darryn Ross no longer existed as far as he was concerned.

Riding beside him, her back straight, her hands

holding the reins the way the riding master had taught her at school, Darryn told herself that she hated him. She'd sooner have been left to mope in her room or to wander about alone than this. She could have talked to Kate, or to Ruth. She was gradually changing her ideas about those two women, but she didn't suppose she'd reach any firm conclusions now. She wouldn't have time.

She and Eyre rode along by the river, then crossed it and climbed the bank. They went through a gate into a paddock where, Eyre said, his best breeding cows were pastured. Darryn, who'd brought her camera, took some pictures and wondered what she'd think of when she printed them. Of Cyrilla Goddard, who'd apparently passed the test when it came to what was required of a mate for a Madison? She giggled a little to herself and then sobered down and listened attentively to Eyre who was telling her about beef roads, pasture improvement, water storage. Moon Mountain was fortunate in that there was underground water on the property, which meant they weren't entirely dependent on a capricious and often inadequate rainfall. As well, she learned that the Madisons owned a property on the Barkly Tableland.

"Handy when we're having a bad time in one place and can shift the stock to pastures that are still good on the other property," he said.

Darryn listened and nodded. She was interested, even though he was merely filling in the silence.

And all the while, he didn't say one single word about her departure.

As they rode back to the homestead, Darryn knew that he'd accepted the fact that she was leaving, and he didn't care. He'd tell Kate tonight what had been "decided," and Kate would nod and Ruth would smile sympathetically, the way she'd been doing lately, and that would be that.

The stockmen were riding in from the mustering camp, and Darryn tried to think of her father who had lived and worked here, but somehow it didn't seem real. She'd made a mess of things, she thought, and for the first time she wondered if she should have stayed in Sydney where she had a good job, exactly as her mother had advised her, instead of coming to the outback and fracturing her life.

"What's up, Darryn?" Eyre asked as they rode on towards the horse paddock. "You're looking really down in the mouth. Not regretting the fact that you're leaving tomorrow, are you?"

His voice was mocking and she cast him a narrow look that she hoped conveyed her dislike of him and his company. She told him with a shrug, "No. All I regret is that I wasted my time coming to your famous cattle station in the first place. I might as well have stayed in Alice Springs, as far as I can see."

"That's because you expect everything at once. You want the world to stop for you," he said unfeelingly. "You think I've broken my promise I suppose."

"Well—haven't you?"

"I don't think so. As far as I'm concerned there's loads of time for you to see all you want to see out here and to take a million and one photographs. However, the choice is yours, and as you said last night, I can get along without you."

"And I without you," she said, stung.

"You haven't exactly proved that, have you?" he said sardonically. "Frankly, I thought you had more go in you. Instead of which, you're running away in a huff."

"That's not true," she said quickly. "I'm not running away in a huff."

"Aren't you? Then why the hell are you running away?" Obviously not expecting an answer, he swung down from his horse and then helped her to dismount. Leaving one of the hired hands to take charge of the horses, they walked together towards the homestead. At the paddock gate, his arm brushed against hers, and she reflected that this was the first time he'd come within kissing distance of her this afternoon. Obviously, kissing her was the furthest thing from his mind.

He pushed the gate open and held it for her. "Go on in and get yourself freshened up for dinner, Darryn. I want to see Chris."

Chris. His head stockman, who could have been her father. Darryn nodded and went on through the garden.

Ten minutes later under the shower, she tried to work out logically and sensibly why she was feeling so unhappy.

To begin with, it was a fact that her miraculous visit to Moon Mountain was a fiasco. She'd made no marvellous discoveries about herself and her Dreaming, and now she was left with the feeling that she didn't belong here and that she wasn't wanted. Yet after all, what could she have expected? A big welcome to the long-lost daughter of a stockman who'd left here eighteen or twenty years ago? It was laughable, when she came to think of it. If Eyre had known her real reason for wanting to visit his cattle station he'd never have invited her here.

Which brought her to the second cause of her feeling of unhappiness: she didn't even have a decent haul of pictures. She'd wasted her time and she couldn't blame it on anyone but herself. She wasn't so helpless she needed to be pushed around in a wheel chair.

Thirdly, she'd somehow become more emotionally tangled up with Eyre Madison than she liked. In fact, it was no use trying to fool herself, she was in danger of falling in love with him. And since she knew very well there was no future in that, it hardly made for delight and happiness.

Stepping out of the shower, she wrapped one towel

around her dripping hair, and used another to rub herself dry. Leaving Moon Mountain now, she told her blurred reflection in the mirror above the handbasin, was no more than good sense. It might be a little mean to walk out on Eyre, but he could take it, and it certainly wasn't going to ruin his life. She'd cut her losses and start again in Alice Springs and life would be good. Her rather childish dreams about her father had vanished, but she still knew with absolute certainty that the outback was her place. Eyre could mock at her "affinity" with it all he liked, but it was still there. She looked forward to working for Margo Talbot, and once she was out of Eyre's orbit, she was convinced it wouldn't take her more than a couple of weeks to get him out of her system. It was a purely physical attraction, she assured herself.

Draping the towel around her, because she'd forgotten to equip herself with a robe, she padded back to her bedroom. She felt a whole lot more cheerful now she'd sorted herself out, and she was going to dress up to celebrate.

Chapter Seven

Darryn wasn't quite sure why she went out for a walk after she dressed that evening instead of going onto the verandah to join the others. But Eyre would probably be back by now, she'd taken so long in the shower, and she was in no great hurry to encounter him again. Dinner time would be quite soon enough.

When she'd finished applying her make-up she stood back to examine herself in the mirror. In her white silk chiffon dress and green sandals, her eyes complemented by bronze-toned eye shadow, she looked cool and sophisticated. Not really like Darryn Ross at all. Inside, she was full of uncertainties, and she wasn't looking forward to facing the Madisons, breaking the news that she was leaving in the morning. She had to do it some time soon, of course, and perhaps she was hoping that in her absence Eyre would do it for her, and anything that had to be said would be over and done with by dinner time.

On the evening air, she could hear faint sounds of activity coming from the outbuildings in the direction of the river. Imagine honeymooning there at the height of summer. Not romantic, she thought with a grimace.

Dust and heat and a lot of rough stockmen tramping about and probably cracking jokes. No wonder her mother had chickened out. And she was chickening out too, she supposed, not liking the thought.

She crossed the room to the French doors and looked out at the evening. The sky was huge and beautiful, swarming with great glowing pink clouds whose reflected light dramatised the garden. A faint breeze moved through the trees and she caught the scent of oleander blossoms. It was her last sunset at Moon Mountain, and as if she couldn't help herself she stepped through to the verandah and went down the steps. A flock of chattering parrots flew overhead, dark silhouettes against the golden pink of the sky, and she stared up at them.

I love it, she thought, and began walking, not towards the orange orchard and the river, but in the direction of the home paddock, along the path Eyre had taken her last night.

She soon found that her thin-soled sandals weren't the best kind of footwear for a walk like this, but there was no point in going back to change them. It would soon be dark, and she wouldn't go far.

The softly draped skirt of her dress flowed against her legs caressingly as she started along the path, and soon she saw two men leaning on the fence, talking. One of them, whose back was towards her, was Eyre. The other, his wide-brimmed hat slanted over his eyes, a cigarette hanging from the corner of his mouth, must be the head stockman, Chris. Not as tall as Eyre but of heavier build, he wore a dark brown shirt, narrow-legged black pants, and dusty boots.

As Darryn looked at him, he took the cigarette from his mouth to say something to Eyre, then shifted his weight, raising his eyes to search out Darryn, whose movements must have caught his attention. She felt a kind of shock go through her, a flash of intuitive recognition, as he eyes lingered on her, and her step faltered slightly. Was it Chris—*Beresford?*

She kept walking though her legs were shaking, and he watched her intently, his narrow-eyed glance travelling over her bright hair and slender form in the silky white dress, and then returning to her hair again. Was she imagining it, or did his eyebrows, though heavy while hers were feather-light, have the same curve as hers? Did his dark eyes have the same slight upward tilt as her own? He looked closer to fifty than to forty-three or -four, and he was tough and hard and weathered. Not at all the kind of man who would attract her mother. But twenty-one years ago they would both have been very different.

Eyre turned his head and frowned when he saw who it was his head stockman was staring at. Darryn had the distinct impression that he didn't want her interrupting, but she didn't care what he wanted, she kept walking.

"What are you doing out here, Darryn?" he asked sharply when she was so close she couldn't be ignored. "I'll be back to dinner when I'm ready."

"I know," she said vaguely. "I—I just came out for a walk."

She looked nervously at the man she believed to be her father. He'd straightened up and his eyes, black and hard, were fixed on her for a long moment while she stood holding her breath, waiting for some sign of recognition that didn't eventuate. Without even the glimmer of a smile, he looked away across the paddocks towards the distant line of flat hills. She put a hand to her hair, and the movement seemed to compel him to look at her again. She smiled at him quickly, and this time his eyes narrowed and his mouth curved briefly upward.

"Well, carry on, take your walk," Eyre said irritably. "I'm not going to join you yet."

"I'll wait," Darryn said. She had to find out what the stockman's name was, and she was determined that Eyre would introduce her. She indicated her flimsy sandals and made a rueful grimace. "I've walked far enough in these."

Eyre looked at her impatiently, the expression in his silvery blue eyes saying very plainly that she was a nuisance, and with sudden annoyance, she linked her arm possessively through his and asked outright, "Aren't you going to introduce me, Eyre?"

That left him no choice, and after a barely perceptible pause, he made the introductions.

"This is Chris Beresford, my head stockman, Darryn."

Darryn drew a deep breath. So she was right! Her legs felt weak, and when she heard what else Eyre was saying, they felt still weaker.

"Chris—meet my fiancée, Miss Darryn Ross."

Darryn couldn't believe her ears. His fiancée! She stared at him, stupefied, then tried to collect her senses as Chris Beresford—her father, she reminded herself dazedly—inclined his head slightly.

"How do you do, Miss Ross. And congratulations to both of you. That's great news, Eyre."

Oh, that's really great news, Eyre, Darryn thought even while she was taking in the fact that the head stockman's drawling voice was, a little surprisingly, both pleasant and educated. News was certainly the operative word, and she longed to say so. Instead, she murmured an indistinct "How do you do." It was all she could manage. She couldn't call her own father Mr. Beresford, or even Chris. It was too much right now, and she tried to catch his eye to see if she could read there that he knew who she was. Surely he must know his daughter's name was Darryn, and that, combined with bright red-gold hair exactly like her mother's, should tell him all he needed.

But when he did look at her, it was with polite impersonality, even with indifference, she thought, feeling hurt. He drew on his cigarette and asked, glancing at Eyre, "When's the wedding to be?"

"We haven't decided on that yet," Eyre said glibly. "Have we Darryn?" he added, and she thought she detected a note of mockery in his voice.

She shook her head. She felt helplessly that nothing was quite real. At this minute she didn't know what she wanted most: to get Eyre alone and ask him what he meant by saying she was his fiancée, or to get rid of him so that she could talk to her father. Eyre had certainly spoiled a dramatic and emotional moment for her, as well as creating turmoil in her mind. She knew she couldn't leave Moon Mountain now, or not so soon anyhow, but how was she going to explain that to him? He'd probably think she was staying because he'd called her his fiancée. The situation had been bad enough before. Now it was impossible.

Full of nerves, she stood slightly away from the two men while they resumed their conversation just as if nothing earth-shattering had happened. For them, she supposed it hadn't. Eyre probably found it amusing to have called her his fiancée, but Darryn didn't find it so. Staring at Chris Beresford, she tried to give her entire mind to him, but her thoughts kept returning to Eyre. *Why* had he said that?—when he knew perfectly well she was leaving in the morning?

He reached out and absent-mindedly drew her back to him so that she was compelled to stand there, his arm around her waist, while he and Chris talked about camp horses and scrub cattle and supplies for the muster camp, and she picked up the information that tomorrow they'd be heading out for the Mountain Paddock. Without Eyre, of course.

"Going over to Dwyers' again, are you?" Chris

asked with a slightly crooked smile, and Eyre shrugged and didn't answer.

Dwyers', Darryn thought, her heart sinking. Was he going there again? Did Chris know there was something between Eyre and Ellen? Did he suspect? And was that why Eyre had said that she, Darryn, was his fiancée? She was really beginning to discover what she'd laid herself open to in agreeing to play along with this man who was far too sophisticated for her. Way out of her league, as the saying went.

But Eyre didn't matter to her, she told herself determinedly. It was her father who mattered, and she wished she could say something warm and personal and meaningful to him. Right now. So why didn't she? Why didn't she bring it all out into the open?

Excuse me, Eyre, but this happens to be my father. Could you possibly let us have a moment to make each other's acquaintance? We haven't met in a long long time . . .

Crazy thoughts. She'd never in a fit say those words. But one thing was for sure: She was going to make herself known to her father. If he already knew who she was and for some reason wasn't going to acknowledge her—well, she was sorry, but she couldn't go along with that.

"I'll see you in a day or so, Chris. Okay?"

Eyre's voice broke in on her consciousness, recalling her to reality with a jerk.

Chris nodded laconically and lit another cigarette. As he shook out the match, he inclined his head casually in Darryn's direction, then leaned against the fence, his back to her.

Darryn hesitated, yet there seemed nothing for it but to move off with Eyre. She'd go down to the stockmen's quarters tonight after dinner, she decided, and wondered uneasily what kind of a reception she'd get.

Recalling those hard black eyes, she knew it was quite possible that Chris would be completely indifferent to her. So was it worth it?

Just for a moment she was tempted to do the cowardly thing and go to Alice Springs after all.

Which brought her back to Eyre's introducing her as his fiancée.

Glancing back to make sure they were far enough away to be out of earshot she demanded, "Why did you say that, just now?"

"Say what?"

"That I'm your fiancée. I never agreed to pretend any such thing."

It was rapidly growing dark, but she saw him shrug. "Well, with you rushing out to the paddock as if you couldn't wait to see me, and then hanging onto my arm the way you did, it seemed reasonable enough. Chris would probably have decided there was something going on, at any rate."

"That's absurd!" she exclaimed, with heightened colour. "You—you know I'm leaving here in the morning."

His eyebrows rose. "You're only going as far as Alice Springs," he said enigmatically.

Darryn looked at him suspiciously. "What's that to do with it?"

"We're bound to run into each other now and again," he drawled.

Were they? She didn't think so, and could only conclude he intended to continue using her to protect Ellen Dwyer. All that business about his family and Cyrilla Goddard was merely a blind. He wouldn't pretend to be engaged to Cyrilla, probably because she had parents to watch her interests. Darryn Ross was a different proposition, a girl living on her own a long way from home. She was the bunny, in fact. Perhaps he thought Harry Dwyer would leave his cattle station to someone else if he thought his wife was unfaithful to him—which she most likely was. Eyre was a very persuasive man.

But he wasn't going to persuade her to make a bigger fool of herself than she already had, and under no circumstances was she going to allow it to be believed she'd agreed to marry him. It was just a shame she couldn't disappear tomorrow as she'd meant to. As it was, it was going to be very embarrassing telling him she'd changed her mind about that, but it had to be done, so she plunged in.

"As a matter of fact, I'm not going to Alice Springs tomorrow after all. That was why I wanted to see you just now," she improvised rapidly, aware of his skepticism. "I didn't want you to break the news at dinner and then have to—to contradict you."

Eyre stopped dead on the path. "Well, well! What's caused this change of heart, I wonder? Why are you staying, Darryn?"

"Not on your account," she said swiftly. Though even as she said it, she knew it wasn't entirely true.

"No? You're quite sure it's not because you've decided you don't want to put an end to our beautiful friendship?"

"It's nothing like that," Darryn snapped. "I'm staying because I might as well get those pictures before I go. It's what I came for in the first place. You were right when you said I was walking out in a huff, but I've got over that now."

"So we're back to square one, are we? Madly in love again."

"If you must put it that way," she said, biting her lip. "But I'm not going to pretend to be engaged to you. You're not to say anything like that to your aunt or to Kate. Or to Cyrilla. If you do I'll contradict you flatly."

"I'll keep that in mind," he said gravely.

They began to walk on again, and he put his arm around her waist and murmured persuasively, "Wouldn't you like to be engaged to me, Darryn?"

"Definitely not," she said, hoping he didn't notice how sensitive she was to his nearness. "Not even for a—a week or whatever you had in mind."

"Suppose I said forever?"

"I don't believe in long engagements," she said smartly.

Her pulse rate had quickened and she was disturbingly aware that deep inside her, she welcomed this excuse to stay on at Moon Mountain, to have Eyre's arm around her, to know that he would kiss her again. Of course it all meant nothing to him. But to her—right at this minute her body was responding to his nearness, and she fished wildly in the dark swirling waters of her mind for some suitable remark to distract both herself and him.

"I want to go out to the muster some time," she heard herself say. "I'd like to get some pictures of the men rounding up the cattle."

"I'll see if I can arrange it," he said absently, and she felt his fingers exploring her hip bone through the silk chiffon dress. It was infinitely sensuous, yet she didn't draw away. "You won't want to stay there overnight, so I'm not sure how it's going to be managed."

"I won't mind staying overnight," she said with nervous eagerness. "I like camping, really I do. And I'm interested in the stockmen—the way they live when they're away from the homestead. Chris Beresford," she hurried on. "Is he married?"

His fingers stopped their exploration. "Now what the hell makes you ask a question like that, Darryn? I can think of only one thing, and I'll tell you right now that you're not going to amuse yourself with Chris Beresford. He's not married, and he's not the marrying kind. He's a loner. Moreover, he's old enough to be your father."

Darryn's tongue played with her upper lip. Suppose she said, "He *is* my father"? He'd ask a whole lot of questions, and she'd be turned inside out. No, until she'd sorted it out with him—with Chris—she must keep quiet.

"I'm fully aware of that," she said ironically. "He's a few years older than you. I don't really know why I asked that question. But he has an interesting face and I suppose I just wondered about him."

"Then keep it to wondering," he said after a moment. His hand moved upwards to her rib cage, and the tips of his fingers sought the swell of her breast.

The next minute his mouth was warmly on hers and he was kissing her. She felt the instant response of her own body as her arms wound themselves around his neck and she gave herself up helplessly to his embrace.

It was nearly dark now. An owl screeched eerily, and Eyre's lips left hers to brush against her temple sensuously as he muttered throatily, "Thank heaven you're staying, Darryn. Alice Springs is a hell of a long way off after sundown."

"What do you mean?" Her voice was husky too, and she felt the stirring of his body and knew that he desired her.

He didn't answer, but his kisses grew more passionate and her responses more ardent, until it reached the point where she knew she must call a halt. With an immense effort of will, she slithered out of his arms and stood trembling, pushing her hair back from her flushed face and listening to the beating of her heart. She was conscious that she'd been dangerously close to losing her head completely. Hang on to your head and your heart, Margo Talbot had advised her. But that was easier said than done.

"Let's get back to the house," she told Eyre, trying

to sound composed. "We're wasting our talents out here. There's no one around to impress."

He agreed to her suggestion without demur, and they walked the rest of the way to the homestead in silence. Darryn knew that she was asking for trouble in staying here. It would mean nothing to Eyre if he broke her heart as well as Cyrilla's. Did Ellen Dwyer know he made love to other women? And did he love her? Or was he planning to marry her for reasons that were purely material and unromantic?

Darryn had no idea, and she couldn't ask.

To her surprise, the next day Eyre offered to set up a darkroom for her.

"It would be no use," she protested. "I haven't brought any of my equipment with me."

"What do you need?" he asked.

"Oh, a whole lot of things. A developing tank—measuring jugs—a thermometer—developer and fixer. Printing paper."

"Okay, you've convinced me. But I'll show you the room that I thought, from my limited knowledge, might be suitable. It opens off the verandah of the store, and it isn't used any more. Are you coming?"

A little unwillingly, she agreed. Kate, who seemed to have completely recovered from her attack of dizziness or whatever it was that had been troubling her, was in the garden, and Ruth and Andrew had both left the homestead long ago.

"I'd like to see some of your work, Darryn," Eyre remarked as they made their way down the side path towards the store.

"It probably wouldn't impress you," Darryn said. "I mostly work in black and white—for myself, I mean."

"Why is that?"

She shrugged. "It gives me more satisfaction. Colour's great for commercial work—studio portraits, parties, weddings, all that sort of thing. But for my own personal work, I prefer black and white."

"You're not totally caught up in commercial photography then," he commented. They'd reached the store, and, going onto the verandah, he took keys from his pocket. "This is the room, at the end here. . . . What's your special field of interest, Darryn?"

Darryn hesitated, uncertain whether he was really interested or not. But it was a safer topic than a good many others he could have chosen, so she went along with it.

"I'm still experimenting, really. I haven't found out yet exactly what I want to do. Maybe I never will. Maybe it's an adventure that will go on all my life. I've been using a camera ever since I was a small child. My grandfather encouraged me, and I started a series of pictures relating to my life when I was about eight. People, places, things that were important to me. Changes in my personal tastes and interests. It sounds rather egotistic I suppose, but it could be of interest to my children—or even to people of a future generation. A sort of very limited social record."

"You have unsuspected depths, Darryn," Eyre commented. He'd unlocked the door but had stood listening to her thoughtfully. "Do you have your collection of photos here?"

She had, as a matter of fact, they were too precious to her to have left them in Alice Springs. But she rather wondered at herself mentioning them to Eyre. As for showing them to him—she thought not. They were too personal. She'd shown them to her grandfather, but to no one else since he'd died.

She looked up, their eyes met, and she looked away again.

"They wouldn't interest you."

His mouth twisted. "You mean you don't want to show them to me. . . . Well, have a look in here and see what you think."

She glanced inside the small room, aware that she'd been rude. But what was the point in responding to his interest in her? It was no more than a form of flirtation, she supposed, and she knew she could fall for it all too easily . . .

Inside the small room there were a bench, a sink with hot and cold taps, shelves, cupboards, a window that could be blacked out— She turned away.

"I suppose it could be converted into a darkroom," she said coolly. "But I'm not really interested, Eyre. I won't be here very long so it's not worth getting excited about."

He didn't answer, and a minute later he locked the door and they returned to the homestead, where he left her to herself.

Well, wasn't that what she wanted? Of course it was! She collected her camera and went to join Kate in the garden.

She liked Kate, and she was beginning to think Kate liked her at least a little. She knew that the bowl of wildflowers she'd found in her room when she came in the previous evening had been put there by Kate. Also, unlike Ruth, who had been definitely put out last night when Eyre announced that Darryn wasn't going to Alice Springs, Kate had accepted the news with approval. Very little had been said, probably because Andrew was at the table, and Darryn had felt rather sorry for Ruth but even more sorry for Cyrilla. The poor girl was in for a pretty thin time. But that wasn't Darryn's fault. Cyrilla was going to have to accept the fact that Eyre wasn't serious about her, and it was a pity she couldn't have been made to realise it without coming all the way from Adelaide.

Darryn was so concerned about Cyrilla that she gave

scarcely any thought to her father. She hadn't gone over to the stockmen's quarters the previous night. Eyre had taken it into his head to talk about music to her, and as it turned out to be a subject in which they were both interested, the evening had disappeared with remarkable rapidity. They both liked opera and Darryn had found several of her favourites in Eyre's record collection.

By the time they'd broken up for the night it had been far too late to do anything but go to bed.

Over lunch, Eyre brought up the subject of her photography again, and Darryn was forced to repeat to Kate some of the things she'd told him that morning, while Eyre for his part repeated his intention of setting up a darkroom for her. It was all no more than a ploy to convince his grandmother that he really was interested in Darryn, and again she thought he was cruel and callous. What would Kate think when, in a week or so, Darryn disappeared to Alice Springs, never to be heard of again?

She went down to the water hole for a swim during the afternoon. Eyre came with her, but they talked very little. Darryn couldn't stop herself from thinking about Cyrilla, who would be arriving with Ruth some time before dinner. She'd said before that she wasn't looking forward to it, and the prospect appealed to her even less now. Eyre seemed totally unconcerned and Darryn told herself over and over that she hated him.

"Get into something really fetching for tonight, will you, Darryn?" he said as they went back to the homestead.

"Why?" she asked flatly, looking up at him, her dislike plain in her eyes. He must have seen it, yet he put his arm around her waist all the same.

"Why do you think? Because I like to see you dressed up, of course."

Liar, she thought, but aloud she said, "I suppose you

think Cyrilla's more likely to take the point if I go to some trouble with my appearance. Is she very attractive?"

"Very," he said with a smile, and drew her a little closer to him. "All my women are very attractive."

Darryn pulled away from him. "Male chauvinist," she muttered, but he merely laughed and told her maddeningly, "Mind you, that carrot hair of yours isn't to every man's taste, but I'm becoming rather partial to it."

He flipped a strand of it, still wet from the water hole, across her cheek and she swished it back angrily. Carrot hair! What a hateful thing to say! He probably loathed it, if he were truthful. Her biggest asset when it came to attractions was no doubt the fact that she had no family hanging around to take an interest in what was happening to her. It would really make him sit up and take notice if she suddenly announced that her father was in the district!

She was still in her room and hadn't finished dressing when she heard a car pull up outside. They were here! Suddenly she was sick with nerves. She'd have given anything to be able to vanish, but there was no place to go. Her fingers trembled as she tied the gold-flecked belt that went with the jade green dress she'd worn the night she had dinner with Eyre in Alice Springs. She knew it suited her, but she looked at her reflection anxiously. Was she wearing too much make-up? She'd applied more eye shadow than she usually wore, in an effort to appear sophisticated. She wasn't sure if it was to give herself confidence or to compete with the kind of girl she believed Cyrilla to be.

Yet however sophisticated Cyrilla was, Darryn felt sorry for her. It would be terrible to arrive at Moon Mountain, your heart full of hope, to find some other girl in possession. Presumably Ruth would have prepared her, but—oh, why had she ever agreed to be a party to all this, she wondered.

She heard Ruth's voice in the hallway and knew Cyrilla was being shown to her room. Then someone knocked on her door and opened it.

Eyre, of course, looking too handsome for words in pale beige pants and a cream shirt.

"Ready, Darryn?"

With one last glance at her anxious eyes and vulnerable mouth, she turned to him.

"Just about."

His silvery blue eyes inspected her, turning her limbs to water.

"You look wonderful." He strode across the room and took her by the arms. "But for heaven's sake, can't you smile? You look as if you're going to a funeral."

Darryn pulled away from him. "What is there to smile about? I told you I was going to hate this."

He looked down at her impatiently. "If that's how you feel you should have left this morning. There's really no need to be so tense. You're not about to witness an execution, you know." He spoke in a low voice and she realised that Cyrilla's room was opposite hers.

"It might seem like an execution to Cyrilla," she said, keeping her voice low too. "You wouldn't know—and you wouldn't care. You—you don't have a heart, do you, Mr. Madison?"

His lips curved quizzically. "Oh, Mr. Madison has a heart, Miss Ross. I thought you'd already discovered that. Feel it beat—" He took hold of her hand and held it against his muscular chest. Instantly, feelings she didn't want to know about were fired in her and she snatched her hand away fiercely. She stood quivering, her back to him, her head lowered, her palms pressed down on the smooth cool surface of the dressing table.

"As for Cyrilla," he murmured from so close behind her that she could feel the warmth of his breath on her nape, "she'll accept the inevitable gracefully, once it's been made plain to her."

Darryn's head remained lowered. It seemed grossly unfair to her that she should have the task of convincing Cyrilla that Eyre was lost to her. Why couldn't Ellen Dwyer be the one to do it? After all she was the one he loved . . .

She raised her head a little. Eyre was prowling round the room restlessly and she watched him through the mirror.

"You think it's so easy, don't you? You don't seem to understand that people can't just—cut off their feelings like that."

He stopped pacing and came to stand behind her.

"Can't they? What do you know about it, Darryn?" Their eyes locked in the mirror and after a moment, Darryn's lashes fell. She was conscious of the rise and fall of her breast, and she knew how much this man could affect her merely by being near to her. It was impossible for *her* to cut off her feelings. For him.

She heard him move, felt his arms come around her, his hands cup her breasts—

"You're not as uninvolved with me as you like to pretend, are you, Darryn?" he murmured, his mouth trailing hotly down the side of her neck.

In the glass, Darryn saw the quick flush that stained her cheeks, felt a swift upsurge of desire engulf her, and despaired of herself. With a movement that was almost violent she broke away from him and said angrily, "Leave me alone! It's—it's time we went to find the others."

"I suppose it is," he said after a moment. "We'll resume our discussion some other time."

The others were in the sitting room when Darryn and Eyre went to join them.

Cyrilla, Darryn discovered, was not supersophisticated, but she was certainly very attractive, and she felt an instant and unexpected spasm of jealousy. She wore an expensive-looking sleeveless white dress and her make-up was subtly stunning, relying mainly on lip gloss and eye shadow. She had dark brown hair that was short and shiny, and her figure was curvaceous and decidedly sexy. Dark amber eyes looked curiously at Darryn, who had the uncomfortable feeling that she was overdressed, that she was overemphasising the fact that she was the girl Eyre had fallen madly in love with.

"Darling," Eyre said, his arm around her shoulders, the warmth of his flesh through the cream silk shirt he wore sending messages along her nerves that she tried to ignore, "this is an old friend of mine, Cyrilla Goddard. Cyrilla—Darryn Ross."

The two girls smiled and murmured. Darryn wondered how Cyrilla liked hearing herself described as an old friend. If it hurt, she hid it well. Ruth, sitting up very straight, her face flushed, dispensed cold drinks from the tray one of the house girls had brought in, while Kate sat a little apart, saying nothing and apparently perfectly at ease.

"It's really weird to be here at last," Cyrilla remarked as she accepted a drink from the tray. "I've heard so much from Eyre about Moon Mountain, and now I'm finding out what it's all about. It's a lovely old house!" She smiled at Kate and then at Darryn. "How are *you* liking it here, Darryn? From what Mrs. Nash tells me, nothing's going to drag you away. You must be rivetted. But there's definitely a shortage of men, isn't there?"

Meaning exactly what? Obviously, that both she and Darryn wanted Eyre. Darryn couldn't think of a thing to say, and it was left to Eyre to say pleasantly, "Well, I'm taking Darryn to the muster out near the mountain tomorrow, Cyrilla. You're welcome to come along too if you want to. There's definitely no shortage of men out there."

"Great," Cyrilla said at once. "I'll be in that. I wouldn't miss it for worlds."

Darryn's spirits sank. So there was to be no escaping Cyrilla. But why on earth had Eyre given her that invitation? She couldn't blame the girl for accepting it, though if she only knew it, she didn't have a hope when it came to Eyre. But she probably regarded Darryn as an interloper and intended to edge her out.

Oddly enough, though she'd felt sorry for Cyrilla before, now that she was actually here Darryn was almost fiercely determined to show her it wouldn't be as easy as she thought to win Eyre over.

And of course it wouldn't be. But that was because of Ellen Dwyer. It certainly wasn't because he was in love with Darryn Ross . . .

Chapter Eight

Next day after lunch, they left for the Mountain
Paddock in the four-wheel drive.

Eyre had spent the morning in the office doing
bookwork, and Darryn had wandered off with her
camera, leaving Cyrilla in the company of Kate and
Ruth. How long they were to stay at the muster
depended on how much the girls were enjoying themselves, but Darryn didn't care whether Cyrilla enjoyed
herself or not. She for one was determined to stay long
enough to make a good strong contact with her father.
Eyre could look after Cyrilla for all she cared, so long
as she wasn't lumbered with her.

They drove through vast paddocks where cattle
meandered under the trees or drank at the bores, and
gradually the low crumpled line of mountains, away
beyond the spinifex and Mitchell grass, came closer.
Eyre said it had been named Moon Mountain by some
pioneer of long ago who'd perhaps been impressed by
its remoteness and unreality.

The violet haze on the skyline turned to indigo and
then to red, until finally the mountains appeared as
great jumbled piles of huge red rocks. Ghost gums and

131

clumps of pale spinifex grew out of the cracks and
crevices, softening the starkness into a primitive beau-
ty. Darryn found the colours breathtaking, and when
they stopped for the cold drinks they'd brought from
the homestead, she relaxed on the sandy ground in the
shade of the trees, awed by the immensity of Eyre's
cattle run and by the vastness and silence of this land.
A few parrots flew chattering overhead, and a long way
off cattle moved slowly, otherwise the emptiness was
complete.

Eyre talked informatively to Cyrilla in the friendly
way of a host, but Darryn, her glance settling on him,
scarcely listened. She fell into a kind of daydream and
was completely lost until suddenly she became aware
that Cyrilla was regarding her steadily, her dark amber
eyes not exactly hostile but definitely calculating, as if
she were trying to assess what kind of an opponent she
had in Darryn.

Darryn dragged herself guiltily out of a fantasy she
didn't dare to remember. If Cyrilla only knew, she
didn't need to worry about her at all. But Darryn was
decidedly worried—about herself. She'd managed to
keep her thoughts at bay all day, but just now, listening
to Eyre's voice, letting her eyes dwell on his strong
masculine face and mobile mouth, all the disturbing
feelings she'd experienced when she woke early in the
morning had come swarming back to bemuse her.
She'd done exactly what Margo Talbot had warned her
against doing, and fallen in love with him. That was
why she'd felt so aggressive towards Cyrilla last night.

Eyre was making fools of them both, she thought
wearily, and when Cyrilla wandered away to walk
under the trees by herself, after Eyre had politely
refused an invitation to accompany her, she told him
vigorously, "I think you're contemptible, Eyre."

He'd been leaning back on his hands, and now he
straightened up and looked at her in surprise.

"More compliments? What have I done this time? Or do you think I should have trotted off with Cyrilla like a good dog?"

"As if you didn't know," she bit out. "Being so nice to Cyrilla—inviting her to come to the muster camp with us—"

"What did you expect me to do, for Pete's sake? If you want to know, the main reason I asked her along is because it will be more pleasant for you, with all those men around."

"More *pleasant* for me! How do you think I feel?" Darryn exclaimed.

"I'm not sure," he said with maddening calm. "I seem to remember we were going to have another talk about your feelings when the opportunity came up. Which it hasn't yet." He looked at her with a lazy smile as he spoke, his eyes moving from her eyes to her mouth, where they lingered deliberately. Darryn's heart beat faster and she felt her blood stir, but she wasn't going to succumb to his charm.

"You're impossible," she exclaimed jumping to her feet. "You know perfectly well I meant how I feel about poor Cyrilla. I'm not going to find it pleasant to see you—snubbing her."

"Have I been snubbing her, Darryn? I thought I'd been perfectly friendly and natural. Unless you count my refusal to go off with her and leave you by yourself. In which case it would have been you I was snubbing, wouldn't it? And believe me, Darryn, I'd never do that. So I wish you'd show your gratitude by being a little more agreeable."

Darryn ignored him, and began to gather up the empty glasses and cans just as Cyrilla sauntered back from a walk so short it had hardly been worth taking.

"It's all so frightfully empty and silent, isn't it?" Cyrilla said, coming to stand near Eyre who'd gotten to his feet.

"You won't say that when we reach the muster camp," he assured her crisply. He offered her a cigarette and snapped on his lighter as she leaned towards him. "How about joining the musterers tomorrow and learning what it's like to hunt half-wild cattle out of the scrub?"

Cyrilla smiled determinedly. She was wearing knee-length cotton pants and a sleeveless white top, and in spite of the heat she looked cool. Darryn knew her own face was flushed, but it was more from her disturbed emotional and mental state than from the high temperature.

"So long as you'll look after me, Eyre," Cyrilla murmured. "What about you, Darryn? But of course you're not a country girl, are you? I suppose a few bulls at close quarters will frighten the life out of you."

"I don't think so," Darryn said coolly. "I have a very strong dash of outback blood in my veins, as a matter of fact. I'm probably a lot less likely than you to be afraid of a few bulls."

She flicked a wary glance at Eyre and somewhat to her chagrin found him smiling sardonically. Well, they must sound amusing—a couple of girls trying to up-stage each other. She wished she hadn't boasted now. She'd never experienced cattle at close quarters, and for all she knew Cyrilla might be right. But if she *was* scared, nothing on earth was going to make her show it. So Eyre could stop being amused in that superior way.

"Obviously you don't know much about me, Darryn," Cyrilla said, amused too. "As Eyre could tell you, I spent the first few years of my life on a cattle station in South Australia. We left and went to the city because there were no sons in the family. But one does have roots, and it all comes back very quickly."

Darryn raised her eyebrows slightly. "You must have been very young when you left the outback, Cyrilla," she said innocently. "Even the emptiness seems to have surprised you."

She turned away immediately after she'd said it, sickened by her own pettiness, and ashamed of the strength of her determination not to let Cyrilla get the better of her. She'd called Eyre contemptible, but she was even more so herself.

The muster camp was in a broad valley in the midst of the low mountains. They came down towards it along a narrow winding track through thick scrub that prevented them from seeing anything at all until the last moment, and then it was all spread out before them. There were permanent yards holding a small mob of cattle, there was a lot of dust, and it looked as though the day's work was nearly ended. A few stockmen were still riding around, but most of them were sitting on their rolled up swags, smoking or drinking mugs of tea.

Darryn looked around quickly, hoping to find Chris. Already she felt tense and her heart was beating fast. Eyre was driving slowly and Cyrilla leaned forward in the back seat, keeping up a running commentary of her impressions which irritated Darryn in her tense mood. She wanted to block her ears, to tell the other girl to keep quiet, and only just managed to keep control of her tongue.

She couldn't see her father anywhere.

"I'm going to put up a tent for you two girls," Eyre said. "Well away from the men and nice and close to the water hole." He slowed down as they came onto the level ground, then cruised along under the trees. "Keep your eyes skinned for somewhere that appeals to you."

Cyrilla let out a squeak a few seconds later. "Here, Eyre! It looks fabulous under those trees."

He slowed down at once. "You're a good picker,

Cyrilla. Level—shady—and the water's no more than twenty yards away. What do you think, Darryn?"

"Whatever you say," she said abstractedly. She was still searching for Chris and beginning to believe he must have been detailed to go somewhere else.

"What about you, Eyre?" Cyrilla was asking. "Where will you be sleeping?"

"Under the stars," he said with a shrug. "The same as the men." He turned to Darryn. "You're satisfied, are you Darryn?"

"Haven't I said so?" she said irritably. She'd scarcely looked at the place, but now she gave it a cursory glance and nodded. "Who's in charge of the muster?" she asked, and was aware of Cyrilla's look of surprise.

"Andrew," Eyre said, frowning. He'd braked to a stop, and raised his hand in salute to a fat man some distance away whom Darryn took to be the cook. He was standing over a huge gas stove attached to a cylinder of gas. His sleeves were rolled up above his elbows and he was inspecting the contents of a large pot. Darryn's glance flitted over him and away. Chris was simply nowhere to be seen.

"I thought you said that Chr—your head stockman would be here to see everything went as it should," she commented.

"Sure, he's somewhere around," Eyre agreed. "But Andrew's the boss in my absence." He climbed out of the Land Rover and opened the door for Cyrilla, but let Darryn get out unassisted. She stood looking around her, and then realised that Eyre had hauled a tent out of the vehicle and was beginning to erect it.

She and Cyrilla did what they could to help, then Darryn asked insistently, "Where *is* Chris?"

"For God's sake, Darryn," Eyre exclaimed. "What's bothering you?"

"She thinks the cattle will go mad and rush the camp

if everybody's not on their toes," Cyrilla said slighting-
ly. She took her smart green suitcase from the car and
asked Darryn, "Aren't you going to get your things?
We'll have to settle in before it's dark. There's no
electricity here, you know."

Darryn swallowed down a smart retort and dragged
out her zippered travel bag. She'd brought extra jeans
and shirts, a change of underclothes, pyjamas, and not
much else. But when Eyre left them to settle into the
tiny tent she soon discovered that Cyrilla was not going
to neglect her looks. She'd brought her make-up kit
with her and was actually planning to change for
dinner!

Well, who cared? Darryn didn't. She was staying
with the jeans and T-shirt she'd worn in the Land
Rover. She looked with amazement at the black
divided skirt and green sleeveless top with gold studs
outlining the scoop neck that Cyrilla was going to
change into—after she'd cleansed her face and brushed
out her hair.

Darryn left her busy with tissues, cleanser and
moisturising cream, and emerged from the tent. Eyre
was talking to some of the stockmen and she drifted in
his direction while her eyes were busy looking for
Chris. She hadn't quite reached Eyre when she saw her
father. He'd just dismounted from his horse and he was
some distance away, yet almost at the very moment she
found him he looked in her direction. His eyes didn't
linger on her, but, determinedly, she walked towards
him.

She hadn't gone far when Eyre caught her up.

"Where are you off to, Darryn?"

"Nowhere," she said guiltily. "I—er—I was wondering what we do about dinner, that's all."

"Hungry, are you?" he said, his eyes gleaming. The
sun was going down in a cloudless sky and the parrots

and cockatoos were making their usual hubbub which added a dramatic quality, an urgency, to matters that otherwise would have seemed mundane.

"Yes, I am hungry," Darryn said. "When do we eat?"

"If you're thinking of consulting the cook, forget it. We've brought our own food from the homestead."

Darryn stared at him. "You mean you and Cyrilla and I are going to eat on our own?"

"Tonight—yes," Eyre said looking at her hard. "Andrew will make it a foursome. Kate—and Ruth—seemed to think that would please you girls."

"It might please Cyrilla, but it doesn't please me," Darryn said, knowing as she said it that she sounded rude. "Why can't we eat with the stockmen?"

Eyre raised his eyebrows. "You can eat with the stockmen tomorrow, Darryn."

"I think it's—it's insulting," Darryn said, flushing. "At least we should ask Chri—the head stockman to join us," she finished angrily.

Eyre hunched his shoulders. "Chris won't be interested. But okay—don't throw a tantrum, I'll ask him. You and Cyrilla can get the food out of the Land Rover and fix it all up. I'll join you presently."

Darryn went back to the tent feeling vaguely troubled.

Cyrilla, resplendent in her divided skirt and pretty top, her make-up exotic in the light of the setting sun, had emerged and to Darryn's amusement was looking around her uneasily, obviously ill at ease. She greeted the news of the evening meal with relief.

"Thank heavens Eyre's so sensitive to my feelings! I must admit the smell of that beef stew is enough to turn my stomach. I don't really fancy lining up with those men to have meat and vegs slurped out onto a pannikin."

"I thought you were used to outback life," Darryn taunted, heading for the Land Rover with Cyrilla close behind. "What did you expect, coming to a muster camp?"

"Exactly what's here," Cyrilla snapped. "But I've never in my life sat down to eat with stockmen, and I'm not going to pretend it's the sort of thing I relish. If you weren't so ignorant of what those men are like you wouldn't be so complacent either. Though perhaps you're not particular about the company you keep."

Darryn turned her back. If she hadn't, she might have said—or done—something unforgivable. Cyrilla stood by and watched as she opened the food hamper, having first erected the folding table she found in the back of the vehicle. She spread out the red and white checked cloth, found the cutlery and the plates, and some covered bowls of salad and cold chicken. There was even a bottle of wine. She thought as she arranged it all on the table that if her father didn't join them, if he stayed over on the other side of the camp with the stockmen, then she'd choke if she tried to eat.

Cyrilla presently condescended to come and set up the folding camp stools and to perch herself elegantly on one and look around her in a superior way. "It's a laugh, isn't it, Eyre saying there's no shortage of men out here. As if one could mix with a lot of stockmen!"

"If that's the way you feel I don't know why you came along," Darryn said coldly.

"Oh yes you do, Darryn," the other girl said. "For the same reason I still came to Moon Mountain when I knew you were here. I don't give up that easily. And I certainly didn't fancy being left behind with those two boring women while you went off with Eyre."

Darryn bit her lip. She felt a little sorry for Cyrilla, but the subject of Eyre was not one she could argue about and she kept silent.

"What's the jackeroo like?" Cyrilla said after a moment. "He should be quite presentable. I hope he's not that big husky brute Eyre's talking to now. I can't imagine chatting to him over a glass of wine, can you? He's obviously all muscle and no brain. One of those men whose whole world consists of outdoor life and cattle. Not my type at all." She shuddered and Darryn coloured hotly. That big husky brute was her father.

She told Cyrilla tightly, "I suppose it doesn't occur to you that Eyre's world consists mostly of outdoor life and cattle. That man he's talking to is Chris Beresford, his head stockman, who happens to be a very intelligent man. And it's too bad for you, but at my suggestion Eyre's asking him to eat with us tonight."

"Then I hope he says no," Cyrilla said with a shrug. "But do you have to be so touchy about it all? I daresay he's a marvellous stockman, but he's still not the kind of man one would mix with socially. I'd never dream of marrying a man like that, and I'm sure you wouldn't either, however broad-minded you like to pretend you are. As for Eyre, you must know only one side of him. I assure you he's very different when he's in the city. . . . Who's this looming up, anyhow? The jackeroo?"

To Darryn's relief, it was Andrew. She didn't know what she might have said to Cyrilla but for the interruption. She introduced them, and Cyrilla was charming. They talked about the camp and the work that was to start at sunup next morning, and Andrew told Cyrilla what he'd already told Darryn—that he didn't intend to live permanently in the outback.

"I like a little social life—and most women do too," he said with a grin. "How are you making out, Darryn? Still in love with the outback, I gather. I heard some interesting news from Chris today," he added significantly.

Darryn's face flamed. She knew at once what Chris had told him, and she stammered out, "Well it—it's not for public consumption. Chris had no right to say anything. You're not to repeat it, Andrew. Please."

The jackeroo gave her a thoughtful look and then nodded slowly. He could have decided that Kate had yet to be told or that the conspiracy of silence had something to do with Cyrilla, but in any event, to Darryn's relief, he didn't ask questions. "I'm sorry. I'll shut up of course."

"What's all the mystery about?" Cyrilla demanded, looking from one to the other of them. "What's this news you heard, Andrew?"

He gave her an apologetic smile. "Sorry, I can't tell you. Just forget it."

Cyrilla was definitely put out but there was nothing she could do about it and after a second Darryn said brightly, "I'll go and see if Eyre's coming."

She hurried away from them, feeling shaken. The long shadows of evening were beginning to fall, indigo and blue across the redness of the ground, and the clumps of spinifex were softened in the sunset light. The parrots and corellas and galahs were screeching, and a flock of bright green budgerigars flew overhead chattering squeakily.

Damn Eyre, introducing her to Chris as his fiancée, she thought angrily. She positively was not lending her name to that to protect Ellen Dwyer, and she was furious with Eyre for his lack of conscience in using her this way. It just wasn't to go any further, as she'd already told him. She didn't think Chris would have said anything to the stockmen, but he'd probably taken it for granted that Andrew already knew.

She forced herself to calm down as she reached the two men, and even managed a smile. Chris gave her a veiled indifferent look that made her shrink inwardly. What had she ever done to deserve to be ignored by her own father? It wasn't her fault she'd never been in touch with him, and he must know who she was. She

felt so shattered by his indifference that she had to fight
to prevent herself from hanging on to Eyre's arm for
support.

"Hello," she exclaimed brightly, smiling at Chris and
trying to show warmth and friendliness in her eyes,
though she didn't have much of a chance since he
avoided looking at her except for one brief glance.

"Good evening," he said formally. It was something
of a giveaway that he didn't use her name—just as she
hadn't used his. He'd have had to call her Miss Ross,
and he couldn't. He dropped the cigarette he'd been
smoking and ground it into the dust with the toe of a
dusty boot.

"Are you two men coming over to eat?" Darryn
asked, still bright. "Everything's ready except for opening the bottle of wine."

"Sorry, but I'm not joining you, Miss Ross." The
way he said it, and the way he used her name this time,
gave Darryn a bitter taste in her mouth.

"But why not?" she insisted. "We—we want you to
come."

He gave her a twisted smile. "I prefer to eat with the
men. I'm more at home there. You'll have to excuse
me." He turned abruptly and walked away.

Eyre took Darryn's arm and she shook it off angrily.
She felt upset about her father and about a number of
other things, and Eyre was to blame for it all. As they
walked across the open space towards the trees where
their exclusive little meal was laid out, she told him
furiously, "You can't have given him a very cordial
invitation. I suppose you think he's not good enough to
eat with us."

"For God's sake," Eyre exclaimed. "What are you
trying to accuse me of? And what does it matter to you
if the head stockman prefers the men's company to
yours? I could have told you that in the first place."

"Could you really? So I suppose you're quite happy about it all. Stockmen—even the head stockman—aren't fit company at your table. Not even out here in the bush."

"Don't be so damned ridiculous," he said, and this time when he took hold of her arm she couldn't shake it off. "What are you trying to do? Dictate who's to eat with whom?"

"No, I'm not. I'm talking about attitudes," she said wildly. "And another thing—Andrew's heard from Chris that you and I are engaged. I—I won't have it. I told him it was a private matter. You talk about me wanting to tell everyone what they can do, but what about you? You'll have to tell Chris it's not true."

"Okay," he agreed with maddening calm. "I'll tell him we had a quarrel and you broke it off. Will that do?"

"You couldn't just tell him you're a liar, could you?" she shot back.

"I'll let you do that," he said, his voice icy now. "I'm sure it would give you a great deal of pleasure. You might like to make it a public announcement."

Darryn wanted to cry. Eyre had let go her arm and was striding ahead so fast that she had either to run to keep up with him or to drop behind. She dropped behind. In fact, she turned back and looked for Chris. Deep in her heart she longed to be able to run to him, to make things happen the way they had when she'd dreamed of finding her father.

But Chris had merged into the crowd of stockmen. It was nearly dark, a fire had been lit, sparks were flying upwards and there was a kind of melancholy in the air. Her eyes filled with tears, her vision blurred. Everything was wrong. Everything.

"Are you coming, Darryn?"

It was Eyre again and this time his voice, instead of

being cold and hard, was warm and gentle. Somehow that made everything worse than ever, because now it was around Eyre she wanted to fling her arms, to have him hold her to him and comfort her. It was a curious feeling, completely asexual, and it had her bewildered.

"Yes, I'm coming," she said subduedly. "I—I had a stone in my shoe."

"Now who's the liar?" he said, pulling her to him.

Darryn drew a deep breath and relaxed against him as they walked on. Unexpectedly, she was remembering what he'd said to her the other day after they'd been riding: You want everything at once, you expect the world to stop for you. Perhaps he was right. She had plenty of time to talk to Chris. There was tomorrow and the next day, and maybe the day after that. She'd do some riding, she'd show him that she was his daughter. Something good was going to happen if she believed it would . . .

"Darryn," Eyre murmured, just before they reached the circle of light cast by a lamp that somebody—presumably Andrew—had lit. "Is it really impossible to add just that little bit of pretence to our relationship? To give it a name? To call it an engagement?"

She moved away from him with a jerk.

"Yes, it is. An engagement's not just a name, it's—it's a promise. And I'm not making any promises of that kind to you."

"You could be right," he said abstractedly.

"Oh, I am right," she said dryly, and almost added, "Ellen wouldn't like it, would she?"

It was romantic sitting out under the stars, and she forced herself to be good company over the meal which was a very pleasant one. The stockmen's fire glowed brightly in the darkness, lighting up the scene as if they were actors on a stage, Darryn thought fancifully. And, of course, she and Eyre *were* actors. . . . Cyrilla did her best to appropriate Eyre, peppering her remarks with constant little asides to him, mostly prefaced by "Do you remember?" Not very subtly, she kept coupling Darryn's name with Andrew's, but it was a losing battle. Eyre was not to be moved, and Andrew knew better than to step out of line.

They'd finished the last of the wine when the stockmen began to move from the fire and disappear in the direction of their swags. Andrew got to his feet too, and stretched lazily.

"Much as I hate to break up the party, it's time I turned in. What are the ladies planning to do tomorrow?"

"We're joining the muster," Cyrilla said confidently. "Eyre's promised to instruct me in the art, so you'd better look after Darryn, Andrew."

"I can look after myself," Darryn said quickly. Her antagonism towards Cyrilla was aroused, but it would actually suit her very well if Eyre occupied himself with someone else. That would leave her free to attach herself to Chris, which she had every intention of doing, and she hoped that by then, Eyre would have cleared up the little matter of their fictitious engagement—if he really intended doing so.

"I'll have a word with Chris in the morning and get him to find a couple of suitable horses for you girls," Eyre remarked, getting to his feet. He looked hard at Darryn and she wondered if that look implied he did mean to see to the other matter as well. "He knows every horse on the property and he'll make sure you'll both be as safe as possible. Though I'll expect you to use your common sense, and not race off on your own," he added. "How about a walk before we turn in, Darryn?"

His eyes, bright in the lamplight, dared her to say no and she got to her feet without answering him. She half expected Cyrilla to pipe up and say she was coming too, but it didn't happen, and she and Eyre moved off on their own.

She felt her nerves tingle as he took her arm, and she knew she was anticipating having him kiss her, make love to her a little. It was madness of course. She was letting herself in for heartache or worse when he dropped her, which he'd do the minute it suited him.

But contrary to what she'd expected, Eyre didn't kiss her, nor did his hand stray from her waist where it lay warm and firm, unnerving her with its very immobility. They walked in silence beneath the trees, and soon he said quietly, "Well, I'll let you get to bed, Darryn. Have you everything you want in the tent? . . . Work starts early in the morning, but I'll wait for you and Cyrilla of course."

"You needn't bother about me," she told him. "I want to take some pictures. I'll be better off on my own."

"We'll see about that," he said a little tersely. "I don't fancy having you get yourself into a spot through not knowing what you're doing."

"That's hardly likely to happen with all those men around," she retorted. "Someone will look out for me."

She could feel his annoyance, but he merely said, "The men have other things to do besides watching pretty girls. . . . I'll see you in the morning. Good night."

He walked away quickly, and Darryn, instead of going into the tent, where a light still glowed, stood staring after him. She was trembling, and she knew to her shame that it was with frustration. She just couldn't understand Eyre Madison. Or herself either, come to that.

In the darkness the fire was dying down, a veil of

smoke scattered with red sparks drifting lazily upwards, and nearby she saw a lone figure standing. It
was Chris Beresford, the head stockman, and the ache
of longing stirred within her. Swiftly, almost without
thought, she went across to him.

He wasn't aware of her coming and for a long
moment she stood in the darkness looking at him. He
was smoking, his head slightly bowed as he stared into
the red heart of the fire. A big, hard-looking man. A
stranger about whose life she knew nothing, understood nothing. Yet he was her father.

Just for the fraction of a second it seemed too
difficult a task to try to make contact with him. She was
afraid of rejection, of hurt; she'd be better off with her
dreams. But it was too late to go back to dreams, and
she wasn't much of a person if she couldn't face up to
reality and accept whatever was handed out to her.

"Chris?" she said quietly, stepping closer to him.

He raised his head and looked at her with those hard
dark eyes that said absolutely nothing and seemed resolutely to refuse her admittance.

"What's the trouble, Miss Ross?"

The indifference in his voice cut her like a knife, and
she swallowed hard.

"I was wondering about tomorrow," she said huskily. "Eyre said you were going to choose suitable horses
for me and Cyrilla to ride."

"Sure, I'll see to that in the morning," he said
agreeably, and returned his attention to the fire.
Darryn stared at him, baffled and hurt. Was he really
trying to freeze her out or was she imagining things?
Well, there was only one way to find out.

"That's not really what I wanted to say to you," she
said awkwardly. She waited for a moment, hoping he'd
help her out, but he didn't look up. He just went on
smoking and staring into the fire, and she burst out

almost accusingly, "You do know who I am, don't you?"

He raised his head and looked at her steadily.

"Yes, I know. You're the girl who's going to marry the Boss."

Darryn bit her lip. She could have denied that, yet she didn't, and strangely it was out of a curious feeling of loyalty to Eyre. She couldn't call him a liar, though he'd suggested she'd probably enjoy doing just that.

"I didn't mean that," she said after a moment. She moved a little nearer to him and flipped her loosened hair across her shoulder. "Don't pretend you don't know. You must. You—you were married to my mother, Helen Westwood. You're my—my father." Tears sprang to her eyes as she said it, but he wasn't moved in the least. He drew on his cigarette, looking at her levelly and unemotionally.

"I'm not your father, Darryn," he said finally, tossing his cigarette into the fire. "We're complete strangers to each other. And you shouldn't be here talking to me at this time of night. You belong over there." He gestured with his head towards the tent, gleaming faintly in the starlight.

She felt such shock at the rebuff that her sentimental tears stopped, and she stared at him stupefied.

"I—I don't know what you mean. I don't belong over there," she burst out. "Of course you're my father! How can you say that you're not? Doesn't it mean anything to you?"

He stroked his chin and lifted his shoulders a little. "How can it mean anything, Darryn? It's too late. You have a father. Hasn't he been good to you—the man your mother married?"

"Yes, but—"

"Then let it be," he interrupted. "Don't stir up trouble for yourself."

"I'm not stirring up trouble!" she breathed. "Can't

you understand? I—I want to know my own father. I've thought about you so often—wondered what you'd be like—"

"Well, now you know, so be satisfied with that and forget it." She opened her mouth to protest but he went on talking, his voice low. "Look—I can see you're a nice girl, Darryn, and that pleases me. But you're Darryn Ross, not Darryn Beresford, and you'd be wise to stay that way. You're engaged to marry a man I respect, and I know you're in love with him. Don't throw a spanner in the works by suddenly announcing you're the head stockman's daughter. How do you think the Madisons would like it?"

Darryn stared at him, her heart beating fast. The Madisons wouldn't like it, she'd known that all along. But what kind of girl did he think she was, for heaven's sake, to refuse to acknowledge her own father? If Eyre had really asked her to marry him, nothing would make her keep quiet. She'd never shelter behind a lie to get what she wanted. . . . But in fact she wasn't going to marry Eyre, though that was something she couldn't explain just yet. Reluctantly, she came to the conclusion that she'd more or less have to keep quiet about her father until the farcical situation with Eyre had come to an end. Which she hoped would be soon. Then things would be different, and it might be possible to establish a good relationship with this difficult man who refused to admit to having any tender feelings for her.

"Well, I suppose I'll keep quiet," she said finally. "But you don't understand. You see—"

Whether she would actually have told him the truth she was never to know, because at that moment Eyre appeared in the firelight, his eyes angry.

"What the devil are you up to, Darryn?" he demanded. "I thought you'd gone to bed and were safely tucked away in your tent."

She stared at him not knowing what to say and Chris came to the rescue.

"Miss Ross is interested in having a ride tomorrow. We were talking about the horses." He lit another cigarette and kicked at the dying fire.

"I don't care what the hell you were talking about, I don't want to know," Eyre said, his voice hard. "But I like to know just where my fiancée is at this time of night. Come on now, Darryn. And this time I'm not leaving you until I know you're in your sleeping bag."

She scarcely managed to murmur good night before he'd taken her by the arm and was hustling her off.

"What did you have to make such a scene for?" she demanded angrily. "Calling me your fiancée when you promised you'd tell Chris we'd—we'd broken it off."

"Just now was hardly the time to do that," he said dryly. "What are you thinking of, chatting up one of the stockmen at this hour of the night?"

"It's not late—and Chris is not *one of the stockmen*." Darryn pulled her arm from his grasp. "He—he told you what we were talking about, but you wouldn't listen. You won't listen if I tell you either."

"Not if you tell me the same lies," he agreed. They'd reached the tent and before she could escape him he'd pulled her roughly into his arms. "Engaged to me or not, for the time being this is where your allegiance belongs—" He bent his head and sought her mouth. Darryn tried to twist her face away from him but in a matter of seconds she was enduring his kisses. Enduring, but all too soon enjoying them . . .

When he released her she was trembling and weak and speechless.

"I'll be sleeping right out here on the ground,

Darryn," he whispered as she went shakily into the tent.

To her relief Cyrilla appeared to be asleep, and she sank down limply on her bedding roll. It was several minutes before she had the strength to grope for her pyjamas and undress. She was sure she wouldn't sleep a wink.

Chapter Nine

She refused to go out with Eyre and Cyrilla in the morning. She'd slept well, contrary to her expectations, and when she woke most of the men, including her father, had ridden out from the camp, though Eyre was still there. By the time she and Cyrilla had breakfasted —Cyrilla sparingly, Darryn hungrily—and fetched their hats, and Darryn her camera, from the tent, their horses were saddled up and Eyre was waiting with them, looking like one of his own stockmen in tight cords, checked shirt and a wide-brimmed hat.

"Ready?" he asked, his aquamarine eyes skimming amusedly over Darryn in her blue jeans and navy T-shirt, and lingering on the white cotton hat she'd jammed on over her bright hair.

"Ready and waiting," Cyrilla said smartly.

"I'm not coming with you," Darryn said, and Cyrilla stared at her.

"Of course you're coming." Eyre's mouth was grim. "I haven't brought you all this way to have you hang around doing nothing."

Cyrilla put her hand on his arm. "Oh, let her do as she likes, Eyre. It's a tall order to expect any girl to ride out in these hills after the wild cattle. I'm pretty nervous myself! I just hope you'll protect me," she finished, looking up into his face and tilting back the becoming green cowboy hat she was wearing with stylish black jeans and white silk shirt.

Eyre took as little notice of her as if she'd been a butterfly alighting on his arm. His eyes were fixed on Darryn's face, and she couldn't look away. Of course she wanted to ride out with him, but what was the point? It was more important to find her father and talk to him again, but the longer she looked at Eyre, the more confused her thoughts became. With an effort, she turned away and glanced towards the scrub, from which a little stream of cattle was emerging at a fast trot, followed by a couple of aboriginal stockmen. She was going to do as she pleased, she told herself firmly, and Eyre could go to the devil. She couldn't see that he was in the slightest danger of being talked into tying himself up with Cyrilla, so why should she be forced to give a display of her—her allegiance?

"Well—what do you intend to do with yourself, Darryn?" Eyre asked, his voice icy.

She looked back at him, widening her green eyes. "I'm going to stay around here and take some photos, of course. What did you think?"

He looked at her a moment longer, then unexpectedly, with a few muttered words she couldn't interpret, he turned his back on her. He helped Cyrilla to mount, swung himself into the saddle, wheeled his horse, and rode away without another word.

Cyrilla followed. She looked very nice on horseback though slightly nervous, and Darryn felt a spasm of pure jealousy, which she brushed swiftly aside. She didn't need to be jealous of Cyrilla, who hadn't a clue as to what was going on. She almost wished *she* were as ignorant. She might be a whole lot happier—though not in the long run.

She watched until the other two disappeared into the

scrub. Cyrilla's horse, aware of its nervous rider, was fidgety, and she wondered how long the other girl would last out. The horse that had been selected for her waited patiently in the shade, and she wandered over to the yarded cattle. Later on, when Chris came in, she might do some riding if she could persuade him to let her go out with him. Her immediate plan was to wait around until he appeared, and while she waited she was going to take some pictures of the stockmen and the cattle. She might as well have some sort of souvenir of her visit to Moon Mountain.

She was soon completely absorbed in watching the activity in the camp and taking pictures of whatever appealed to her. The air grew dustier as the mob of cattle grew and there were a few exciting incidents when a runaway beast had to be chased out of the trees. Darryn watched the procedure with interest, and managed to get some pictures that she thought should be excellent. It was fascinating to see how a good camp horse seemed to know exactly what to do, drawing level with the runaway bullock and shouldering it around until it was under control. The stockmen, particularly the aborigines, were fantastic riders and Darryn was enthralled.

She was so busy edging around to take a picture of one of the riders who was rolling a cigarette with one hand while keeping an alert eye on the cattle he was bringing in to the yards that she nearly got herself into serious trouble. She'd moved further away from the yards than she had realised—in fact she was right out in the open—when suddenly she heard the pounding of hooves and turned swiftly to see a huge red bull coming straight towards her. For a moment she was too shocked to think, let alone to move.

She didn't know what would have happened if one of the stockmen hadn't raced in on his camp horse just in the nick of time and diverted the beast, which, head down, looked ready to charge her. She regained the power of her legs and ran rather shakily to the yard rails where she stood breathing unevenly, watching her rescuer and suddenly realising that the dust-streaked face half-hidden by a forward-tilted hat was her father's.

Oh, wouldn't it have to be, she thought in dismay. She'd so badly wanted to impress him, and now he'd think her a fool, and a frightened fool at that.

He rode over to her an instant later, and she saw that his mouth was tight and he was white around the nostrils.

"You'd better keep out of the way from now on, Darryn," he said, looking down at her from his horse. "It's hardly worth risking what could be a fatal accident for the sake of a few pictures. I don't want to see you kill yourself."

Darryn stared back at him, noting again the way his eyes tilted at the corners, just like her own.

"Why should you care whether I kill myself or not?" she heard herself ask, though she hadn't planned to say any such thing. "You've lived without giving me a thought all these years—I'm just a—a stranger as far as you're concerned—" She stopped, biting her lip, and saw his hard dark eyes flicker. Then he dismounted from his horse and stood a few feet away, lighting a cigarette, his hands unsteady.

"I guess I do care, Darryn," he said after a moment, looking up at her through half-closed eyes. "It's a funny thing about blood."

Darryn felt a curious stirring in her heart and tears flew to her eyes. Was the rapport that she'd imagined would be instinctive and instantaneous beginning to emerge? Her father felt something for her after all, and she was deeply moved. More so perhaps because he seemed so hard and uncaring. But there'd been—tenderness in his voice.

"I'm sorry," she murmured. "I don't want to cause an accident—to myself or to anyone else. I just got so absorbed in what I was doing I forgot to use my common sense."

"Then don't forget again," he said. He smiled at her—really smiled—and their eyes met again, and this time his eyes were not hard at all. They were interested, concerned. She wondered if Eyre had said anything to him yet about their fictitious quarrel, the breaking of their engagement, but she didn't like to ask.

"Why aren't you riding with Eyre this morning?" he asked. "Didn't you like the little mare I picked out for you?"

"I wanted to take some pictures," she said. "And to see you. Couldn't I ride with you for a while now?"

He smiled wryly. "I don't know that that's much of an idea. Eyre will want to find you waiting here when he comes back."

She shrugged. "Then it will be too bad for him. He's taken Cyrilla with him anyhow," she added deliberately, leaving him to make what he liked of that.

"You've quarrelled, haven't you? He told me that this morning," her father said, and she flushed deeply. So Eyre had kept his promise, and she wondered why she wasn't pleased. Somehow she hadn't thought he'd say anything. "Well, don't be too upset, it'll blow over. . . . All right then, you can come with me if you like and we'll see how you go."

"Oh, good," Darryn exclaimed.

She dashed off to where her horse still waited, and a few minutes later, as they rode together towards the scrub, she flushed with pride when Chris told her, "You ride well, Darryn. Where did you learn?"

"At boarding school. I was there for a year while

they—my mother and fa—Richard—were overseas. I haven't ridden for ages, but it must be in my blood. I always thought I must take after you rather than after my mother," she rushed on, pleased that he was riding slowly and was obviously giving her an opportunity to talk to him. "She and I don't have a lot in common. Though we get on quite well," she hastened to add. "Were your people—on the land or something?"

"Nothing like that. Don't get any flash ideas about my parents, Darryn. They were just nice ordinary folks, as far as I know. They both died when I was very young. My father was a part-time musician—a violinist. He worked in a small music shop in Adelaide. Didn't Helen tell you any of these things?"

"She didn't seem to know anything to tell me," Darryn said ruefully. "Perhaps she's forgotten. So who brought you up?"

"My aunt and uncle. I wasn't particularly happy, probably because they were always at each other's throats." He reined in under a tall tree as he spoke, and Darryn reined in too. "We'll stop here for a few minutes if you want to talk. You don't smoke?"

"No." She almost wanted to say, "I wish you wouldn't either," but he wouldn't want a girl of twenty, even if she was his daughter, trying to reform him, so she kept quiet.

"It's a bad habit," he said, lighting up. "I should give it up. . . . Anyhow, I suppose Helen told you that I cleared out from home and came to the bush as soon as I was old enough to leave school."

She shook her head and he went on, "I got work on various cattle stations, roamed around a bit, enjoyed my freedom. I was working here on Moon Mountain when I met Helen at the rodeo in Alice Springs. We fell in love at first sight—rushed off and got married. It was a disaster. We were like two babes in the woods, completely without experience. But strawberry leaves weren't enough for her. She'd been gently brought up, and when she saw the little cottage the Missus let us have she cried her eyes out. She wanted me to go back to the city and we quarrelled for a week. There were no more rose-coloured glasses after that. She ran off back home as soon as she had an opportunity, and I can't say I blame her."

"You must have been brokenhearted when she left you," Darryn said after a moment. "Is that why you've never married again? You haven't, have you?"

"No, I haven't, but that's not why. I'm a loner, I guess. You don't take after me that way! I should never have married, but I was too young to realise it when I met Helen. I like my life the way it is—no responsibilities beyond what I can comfortably handle, no one to tell me I should be more ambitious, to demand anything of me."

"I won't ask anything of you," Darryn said anxiously.

He smoked for a minute or so without speaking and then said slowly, "I was thinking about you last night, Darryn. We're both of us right, you know. You are my daughter, and yet you're not. When the lawyers got in touch with me about the divorce, they said it would be best for me to keep out of your life. I accepted that, and it still holds good now. There's no point in bringing it into the open. It won't do you any good to proclaim our relationship and you know why."

Darryn stared at him, her cheeks flushing. "I'm not ashamed to be your daughter," she said, her voice low, and he narrowed his eyes and looked away from her.

"I know that. But I prefer to stay out of the picture. . . . There's an overseer's job going on Madisons' property on the Barkly Tableland. I'll take it—I mentioned it to Eyre this morning."

Darryn bit her lip. This was crazy—for her father to turn his life upside down when she wasn't even going to marry Eyre. "But—but aren't you happier here?" she stammered.

He shrugged. "One place is as good as another. I didn't come back to Moon Mountain because it's the best place in the world. Things just worked out that way."

"But suppose I don't marry Eyre," she said uncomfortably.

He shot her a hard look. "What did you quarrel about? That overdressed city girl in her green hat? You don't need to worry about her, she's not Eyre's type. She's even more scared of the stockmen than she is of the cattle."

Darryn bit her lip, not knowing what to say. Obviously Chris suspected nothing about Ellen and Eyre.

"It'll mend," her father said. "I've never known Eyre to look at a girl the way he looks at you—real possessive." He laughed a little. "It's a funny feeling being proud of my daughter. I am proud of you, you know. . . . I hurt your feelings yesterday, didn't I?"

"Yes," she admitted.

"I'm sorry about that. I just didn't know how to handle the situation. I don't altogether know how to handle it now," he added with a crooked smile. "But I guess it will sort itself out in time. . . . I think you'd better go back to the camp now, and wait for Eyre, don't you?"

"I don't want to do that," Darryn protested. "Let me come with you—please! I promise I won't make a nuisance of myself."

He gave in, and she spent the next hour or so riding alongside her father, helping him hunt out the cattle, and, thanks to her well-trained horse, not disgracing herself.

A plane was droning overhead as they finally started back to the camp towards lunchtime. Chris stared upward, his hand shading his eyes.

"That's the air ambulance. Looks as if it's going to land at Linette Downs."

"Harry Dwyer?" Darryn exclaimed.

Chris nodded, his face serious.

"I'd reckon so. He's already had a couple of strokes —I've heard the next one could be fatal. He's too young to die. Fifty-two. It's said to be a dangerous age. Eyre will be concerned. He and Harry have been good mates for a long time, despite the difference in years."

Darryn felt a chill come over her heart. She couldn't pretend to feel anything for Harry Dwyer personally since she'd never met him, but she wouldn't have been human if she hadn't thought of the consequences of Harry's death as they affected Ellen and Eyre—and herself.

"What will Ellen do?" she asked, her voice shaking, and was shocked when her father laughed shortly and mirthlessly.

"You've met Ellen, have you?"

"Not really. Only once—with Eyre at the rodeo," Darryn said making her statement deliberately vague. "Do you know her?"

"Oh yes, I know Mrs. Dwyer," he said, his voice hard. "She's been hounding me for the past six months to take a job at Linette Downs. A great promotion."

"Why didn't you take it?" Darryn asked, not understanding.

"Because I don't like her. As for what she'll do—she can look after herself, I think." He said nothing more, and Darryn thought bitterly, Eyre will look after her . . .

They rode on. The plane could scarcely be heard now and Darryn's nerves were quivering. Eyre would have heard that plane too, known as Chris did what it meant—

A few minutes later they came out of the hills into the camp in the valley. It was swarming with men and cattle, the air was full of dust and smoke, and suddenly, Darryn felt utterly weary. She looked for Eyre but found only Cyrilla, seated on a camp stool alone in front of the tent.

After she'd thanked Chris for looking after her and left him to deal with the horses, she hurried over to the tent. Cyrilla was patting moisturiser into her skin, and although she looked exhausted, Darryn couldn't help noticing that her white silk shirt was scarcely soiled, and that her expensive jeans were only a little creased. The part that showed the most wear and tear appeared to be her good humour, for her greeting to Darryn was irritable.

"Where have you been?" she demanded. "You look as if you've been dragged backwards through the spinifex."

"I feel a bit that way," Darryn agreed with a laugh. "I've been up in the scrub after cattle, the same as you. Where's Eyre?"

Cyrilla widened her beautiful amber eyes. "Hasn't anyone told you?"

She paused infuriatingly and Darryn dragged off her dusty hat and shook her hair out, running her fingers through it. "No. I've just come back to the camp."

"You heard that plane going over I suppose?"

"You mean the air ambulance?"

"That's right. . . . Well, Eyre's gone off in the Land Rover to Linette Downs to see if he can be of any help. There's a sick man there—a particular friend of Eyre's—"

"Harry Dwyer," Darryn spoke almost absently. A particular friend of Eyre's. That seemed to be the general impression. Frankly, Darryn didn't believe a word of it. Hating the bitterness and ugliness of her thoughts, she said quickly, "I hope it's not bad news."

Cyrilla shrugged. "I wouldn't know. At all events, you and I are to leave this afternoon. Some stockman's to take us back to the homestead in Andrew's moke. I said I'd drive, but Eyre seems to think we'd get lost."

"We're leaving this afternoon?" Darryn, who'd been about to put her camera in the tent out of the sun, stared at Cyrilla incredulously. "But why? I don't want to leave yet!"

"Well, I do," Cyrilla said determinedly. "You may be enjoying yourself, but I've had about all I can stand and I told Eyre as much. All I want is to get back to the homestead where at least we'll be comfortable, even if the company bores us to tears."

"You mean it was your idea?" Darryn said slowly.

"More or less," Cyrilla agreed. "But don't worry— Eyre was all in favour of sending us back. He was ropeable when he heard what you were doing."

"What do you mean—he heard what I was doing?" Darryn exclaimed.

"He expected you to be there, taking pictures or something when we came back," Cyrilla said raising her eyebrows. "I really don't think he appreciates the way you run around in circles after that burly head stockman of his, Darryn. Don't tell me you're not aware of it."

Darryn flushed. "Don't be absurd. Just what are you implying?"

Cyrilla had produced a brush and was drawing it vigorously through her shining hair. "Darryn—are you pretending or do you really not know that Eyre is jealous of that man?"

"Jealous? Of course he's not," Darryn said faintly. "What—what on earth gave you that idea?"

"Eyre did. We had a long talk this morning. It's just

as well you didn't come with us because we had a lot to
say to each other."

"Did you?" Darryn wondered what was coming
next, but Cyrilla was in no hurry to go on. She got up
and brought the water bottle from the tent, then
proceeded to pour herself a mugful of the cool water.
Darryn narrowed her eyes and looked across at the
stockmen, smoking and talking as they waited for
lunch. One or two of them were seeing to their horses,
a couple more were still working around the holding
yard. The cook was standing over his gas stove and it
looked as though the meal would soon be ready. She
discovered Andrew talking to Chris, and let her eyes
dwell on her father as she thought of their long
conversation of the morning.

Something good was going to come out of her visit to
Moon Mountain after all—something lasting. She
hadn't found the elusive thing she'd sought and that
she'd called her Dreaming, but she'd found something
better. Her father. And if she'd been silly enough to fall
hopelessly in love as well, she'd just have to get over it.
She hoped that Chris *would* move to the Barkly Tableland. Then she'd be able to visit him sometimes,
perhaps. Because she'd never be able to come back to
Moon Mountain. Never . . .

"What's the matter, Darryn?" Cyrilla asked. "You
look pale. Put your hat on again, for goodness' sake,
and sit down in the shade."

Wordlessly, Darryn did as she suggested, after fetching another camp stool from inside the tent.

"I dread the thought of what we're going to be
expected to eat," Cyrilla went on. "Andrew's promised
to bring something over here for us, anyhow. Or do you
intend to race off and join the head stockman, by any
chance?"

"No, I—I'll have my meal here with you," Darryn
said.

"Good. I was going to tell you—Eyre and I each had a confession to make. We got that over this morning. Shall I tell you my confession first?"

"You don't have to tell me anything, Cyrilla," Darryn said. She reached for the water bottle and poured herself a drink. What with the heat and the dust, she was parched.

"Oh, I want to tell you, Darryn, I think it's only fair. After all, you must have been wondering if I'm in love with Eyre. Isn't that so?" Cyrilla asked.

"I—I suppose so," Darryn murmured uncomfortably.

Cyrilla nodded. "I thought so. Well, he is a fabulous man, and we really got together last time he was in Adelaide. We had some super times, and I'll admit I hoped he'd ask me to marry him. When old Mrs. Madison sent me an invitation to visit Moon Mountain I jumped at the chance." She paused and grimaced. "Now of course I can see why Eyre didn't talk marriage to me. He knew I wouldn't be bowled over by the outback. I'm just about screaming with boredom already. I'll admit the house is lovely, but what else is there? And Eyre's so—different here in his own setting from the way he was in Adelaide. Oh well," she finished with a shrug, "there are plenty more men in the world, thank heaven."

Not for me there aren't, Darryn thought somberly. But it was a relief to know that Cyrilla felt this way, and that there'd be only one broken heart lying around— Darryn Ross's—when Eyre announced his intention of marrying Ellen Dwyer.

"So far as I'm concerned," Cyrilla continued after a moment, "anyone who wants Eyre can have him and all that goes with him—Moon Mountain and the heat and the flies and the dust. And Kate Madison as well. How do *you* feel about those things, Darryn?"

Darryn smiled vaguely. It was like asking someone

how she felt about having to put one foot in front of the other in order to walk. No matter what went with marriage to Eyre Madison, she knew she'd accept it if she had the chance. But the point was, she wouldn't have the chance, and she supposed she should be thankful that at least she was aware of that. If Margo Talbot hadn't clued her up, she just might have been living in a fool's paradise.

On the other side of the camp, she could see Andrew painstakingly piling up plates of food to bring across to her and Cyrilla, and she felt irritated. How much more friendly it would be for the two of them to join the stockmen. Yet a moment's thought told her that the stockmen might well feel ill at ease with two girls in their midst, so perhaps Cyrilla was right. Except that Darryn would have liked to sit with her father.

". . . So that was my confession to Eyre," she heard Cyrilla say.

Darryn gave her a puzzled look. "I'm sorry—I didn't quite get it. What did you confess?"

"That I wouldn't marry him," Cyrilla said widening her eyes. Then unexpectedly she laughed. "Well, all right, he didn't ask me. And that brings me to *his* confession," she added.

Darryn felt a tremor run through her. Was Cyrilla going to tell her she knew about Ellen Dwyer after all? But she wasn't to find that out yet, because at that moment, Cyrilla exclaimed, "Oh look—here comes Andrew with our ghastly lunch!"

"Hi, girls," Andrew said. "Are you going to be able to wrap yourselves around this delicious offering?"

Cyrilla grimaced and then, as she looked at what was on the plates, her expression brightened. "It doesn't look too bad. Grilled steak!"

"And salad," Andrew said triumphantly. "We eat well on Moon Mountain. Well, get stuck into it, girls. I understand Stan's to drive you back to the homestead when you've eaten. Boss's orders," he added, looking at Darryn thoughtfully. "Sounds as if it could be rotten news about Harry Dwyer. I can't join you for lunch; I'm having a powwow with Chris. I'll come and wave good-bye when you're leaving. Okay?"

"Okay," Cyrilla agreed blithely, and Darryn managed a smile.

"He's quite a pet, that man," Cyrilla murmured as Andrew moved off. "But still pretty boring. I really think I'm a complete convert to city types as from now. I gather you haven't made up your mind, Darryn."

Darryn blinked. "What do you mean?"

"Well, I was about to tell you that Eyre confessed he's madly in love with you but that he hasn't persuaded you to marry him yet."

For just a second Darryn couldn't believe her ears, and then her common sense came to her rescue. If Eyre had told Cyrilla that it was merely to keep up the fiction of their romance. And he'd have said it before that air ambulance flew across the sky.

"No comment?" Cyrilla said dryly, and Darryn shook her head.

They ate their meal, and this time Cyrilla had more appetite than Darryn. In no time at all, they were in the moke being driven back to the homestead by a taciturn stockman called Stan. Darryn didn't even have an opportunity to explain to her father what was happening, though no doubt Andrew would have told him. She had no idea when she'd see him again.

The news of Harry Dwyer had already reached the Moon Mountain homestead over the radio transceiver when Cyrilla and Darryn arrived.

"Where's Eyre?" Ruth demanded as they brought their luggage onto the verandah, and Cyrilla explained that he'd driven over to Linette Downs to see if he could be of any help.

Darryn went inside to her room. She felt sick and

heartsore and she had some thinking to do. She hated the situation she was in more than ever, and she didn't like herself very much either. She wasn't thinking of Ellen, or of Harry or of anyone else. Just of herself. If Harry Dwyer died, as it seemed probable he would, then she wanted no more to do with Eyre. She had to get out of his life. And the prospect was unbearable. Yet she had known all along it must happen, whether Harry died or not. So what had she been hoping somewhere so deep in her subconscious that she'd pretended she wasn't hoping at all?

She took a shower, and as the lukewarm water ran caressingly over her body, she remembered what Cyrilla had said: Eyre says he's madly in love with you but he hasn't persuaded you to marry him yet. How she wished that were true! Yet how could she imagine herself in love with a man who was so glib, who would stop at nothing to keep the eyes of his small world off his passion for his neighbour's wife?

I hate him, she told herself vigorously as she combed out her curly red-gold hair in front of the bedroom mirror a few minutes later.

Someone knocked at the door and Cyrilla came in and slung herself down on the bed where she lay watching her.

"You're really very clever, Darryn."

"What on earth are you talking about?" Darryn asked, mystified.

"Slipping off the way you did just now—leaving me to listen to those two women waffling on about poor Ellen and who's going to run Linette Downs and whether Eyre's going to take on a double burden. You'd think Harry Dwyer was already dead. I might sound heartless but I don't know the guy and I'm just not interested. I'd rather hear about what you're planning to do."

She sat up on the bed and let her glance run over

Darryn in her short towelling robe, her hair still hanging loose and damp about her face. *"Are* you going to marry Eyre?" Doesn't the thought of having that old lady always there, reminiscing on and on until you could scream—doesn't that fill you with horror? Oh, I know there's a lot of talk about her going to Adelaide to live with Mrs. Nash, but I don't believe she has the least intention in the world of doing that. What's more, she'll probably live forever."

Darryn moved across to the wardrobe to find something to put on. "I like Kate," she said coolly.

Cyrilla laughed shortly. "Then you must be martyr material. When I marry I intend to have my husband to myself. No interference from mothers or grandmothers or aunts." She got up from the bed and drifted aimlessly around the room. "There's not a damned thing to do in this place. I wish Eyre would hurry up and come home. I intend to get out of here the minute I can."

She wandered off and Darryn went on dressing. She didn't think Eyre would hurry back. He'd be—looking after Ellen. She wondered how Ellen would get on with Kate, or if, like Cyrilla, she'd find the old lady a bore. Cyrilla was probably right in saying that Kate didn't want to leave, but she knew that if she were marrying Eyre, she wouldn't mind one little bit . . .

"Did you have an interesting time at the muster?" Kate asked at dinner, and Cyrilla sent her a bored look.

"I wouldn't say I found it rivetting, though Darryn might have different ideas. I don't quite know what she did with her time—she spent most of it with the head stockman."

Darryn looked down at her plate. Was that remark made deliberately to earn her Kate Madison's disapproval? Or was it entirely innocent?

"And what did you learn from the head stockman, Darryn?" Kate asked, her eyes sharp.

"Oh, a lot of things." Darryn raised her head and

looked Kate straight in the eye. "He's a very interesting man. I had a great time riding around with him after the cattle."

"Did you indeed? Well, you may not believe it, but I've taken part in many a muster myself. I'm far too old for that now, to my regret."

Ruth laughed gently. "You certainly are, Mother. You shouldn't even be living in this part of the world at your age and in your state of health."

"Oh rubbish, Ruth! I'm perfectly healthy," the old lady said. "I intend to see Eyre married before I leave here. You know that." She turned to Cyrilla and asked her bluntly, "Would you like to spend the rest of your life on a cattle station, Cyrilla?"

"Definitely not," Cyrilla said, her eyes hard. "I've grown used to exercising my brain in the city—to mixing with a variety of people. This place is too empty for me."

Kate sniffed. "What you find in a place depends on what you bring to it. . . . What did you tell me your father's occupation was, Darryn?" she asked suddenly, completely changing the subject. "Didn't you say he's an academic of some sort?"

"An academic!" Cyrilla exclaimed before Darryn could answer. "Why—I thought you said you had some sort of a country background."

"My stepfather's a university lecturer," Darryn said, her colour high. "My—my mother's divorced, and I've been living with her and my stepfather. My father is from the country." She bit her lip and waited for Kate's next question—which was going to be, "And what does he do in the country?"

But to her relief Kate didn't ask it. She merely nodded and returned her attention to what she was eating.

The news came over the radio transceiver next morning that Harry Dwyer had died the previous afternoon on arrival at the hospital. Later on, over the open session during which news was exchanged amongst the station wives, Ruth let it be known that the party at Moon Mountain had been cancelled, because of Harry's death. Darryn knew there was another reason for that as well, that Ruth had at last had to accept that Cyrilla was not going to marry Eyre.

There was a general air of quietness about the household, but Darryn for one was aware of Cyrilla's impatience with everything. She didn't actually complain but her every word, her every action proclaimed that she was bored, bored, bored. Darryn's attempts to persuade her to come for a swim in the water hole failed, and eventually she left her to sulk alone and spent a relaxing hour in the garden with Kate, where she heard about various native plants Kate planned to cultivate.

"It's a pity you don't drive, Darryn. We could go out on a plant-gathering expedition together. Eyre's forbidden me to take the car out, unfortunately."

"I'll have to learn," Darryn said, and then broke off, embarrassed at the implications of her words.

"You will indeed," Kate agreed with a smile. "When things have quietened down we must speak to Eyre about it."

Darryn let it go at that. She didn't want to get into a discussion of her future.

It was another day before Eyre came back, and Darryn, who'd imagined he must have been at Linette Downs consoling Ellen, discovered he'd been at the camp. He knew of Harry Dwyer's death, he looked weary, and he hadn't much to say.

The funeral was to be the following day, and Eyre was flying down to Alice Springs.

"What about you, Ruth?" he asked as they all sat on the verandah where tea and scones had been set out. "Are you ready to go back to Adelaide yet?"

"No, I shan't go yet," Ruth said. "I told Frank I'd be away at least a month, and no matter what Mother says, she can do with me here for that little extra while. I've cancelled the party by the way. It seemed the best thing to do under the circumstances."

"Quite right," Eyre agreed. He glanced across at Cyrilla, slumped in her chair, sipping her tea. Darryn had already noticed she'd been staring at Eyre fixedly, and she wondered whether she was very much in love with him. Was she more cut up about the way her visit had turned out than she pretended? Or did she really not fancy living at Moon Mountain?

"What are your plans, Cyrilla?" Eyre asked courteously.

"Oh, I'll get out of everyone's hair and go back to Adelaide," Cyrilla said with a shrug. "That's if you can give me a lift in the plane."

"Of course. Whatever you want."

Darryn moistened her lips. She'd scarcely spoke to Eyre since he came back. "I'd like to come too, Eyre."

Their eyes met and Darryn looked hastily away, unnerved by what happened to her simply through eye contact. She was reduced to jelly—helpless.

"We'll talk about you later," Eyre said, and immediately changed the subject.

When Darryn excused herself a few minutes afterwards and went to her room to shower and dress for dinner, Eyre followed her. She'd kicked off her sandals and taken off the little gold watch her father—no, *Richard,* she reminded herself—had given her on her eighteenth birthday, and she was just about to strip off her dress.

"Darryn—may I come in? You're decent, aren't you?"

Immediately her heart began to pound. She slid her feet back into her sandals and glanced hastily at her reflection, to discover her eyes had darkened and her mouth was trembling. "Yes—come in," she said shakily.

He shut the door behind him, then crossed the room to her and put his arms around her and looked down into her face.

"There's no need for you to leave yet, Darryn. I'll only be in Alice for a day. You can wait at least until Ruth's gone, can't you?"

His aquamarine eyes held hers for a long moment and then her gaze moved to the firmness of his mouth with its curving slightly sensual lower lip and she felt herself tremble inwardly. He'd locked his hands behind her back and she leaned against them, straining her body away from his, afraid of what a closer contact might do to her.

"There's no point in my staying any longer," she said, forcing herself to speak coolly. "Cyrilla's leaving, she told everyone at dinner the other night that she—she's not going to marry you. You only wanted me here to—to show you weren't interested—that way—in Cyrilla. Though I'm sure it wasn't necessary," she finished with a rush.

"Maybe it wasn't," he agreed. "But aren't you forgetting something else?"

"What?" Her lids flew up and she felt a shock that was almost physical at the impact of his eyes and the way he was looking at her.

"Your pictures, Darryn," he said quizzically, and she flushed painfully.

"I've taken all the pictures I want," she stammered, aware that he was gently drawing her closer. She half closed her eyes and with a little shiver felt his mouth come down to hers and move there sensuously, his lips warm and caressing against her own.

"Don't go yet, Darryn," he murmured. "We haven't got to know each other yet—not nearly well enough."

"Well enough for what?" she stammered.

"Don't you know, Darryn?" he said softly, and she darted one swift frightened look at him and then lowered her lashes again.

"I—I have to get back to Alice Springs. Mrs. Talbot doesn't expect me to stay away indefinitely." She suddenly struggled free of him, haunted by an image of Ellen Dwyer, complete with drooping hat—Ellen who should never have married a man so much older than herself, who was now a widow—and who could look after herself, Chris had said. She probably wasn't shedding any tears, and Darryn hated the thought of Eyre coming back from the funeral—spending his days at Linette Downs—"helping out"—while she, the decoy, stayed on at the homestead, letting everyone think he was in love with her.

"It's no use trying to persuade me to stay," she managed to get out. "I—I want to go back to my own life again."

"Very well," he said slowly. "Then we'll do it your way, Darryn. You can fly down to Alice Springs with me in the morning. Good night."

The door closed behind him and Darryn sank down on the bed, her face in her hands.

Chapter Ten

In an unimaginably short space of time Darryn was back in Alice Springs. Cyrilla, who had arranged to take the evening plane for Adelaide, waited in the car Eyre had hired for the day while he accompanied Darryn into the motel where she'd stayed before.

"Don't bother about me," Darryn told him stiffly when he insisted on seeing her to her unit. "Cyrilla's waiting for you."

"Forget about Cyrilla. I want to have a word with you before we part."

Before we part. Darryn wished it were all over. The partings at Moon Mountain had been bad enough. Kate had kissed her and said good-bye as though she expected to see her again shortly, and even Ruth had been pleasant, though Darryn had thought, a little cynically, that it was mainly because she was leaving. It had also occurred to her that Ruth might see her in a different light now that Cyrilla was no longer regarded as a likely wife for Eyre. She might not have been so pleasant if she'd known that Darryn was Chris Beresford's daughter, of course!

Now, inside the motel room, Eyre stood looking

down at her, his eyes sombre and unreadable. In dark trousers, a white shirt and black tie—his jacket was in the car—he looked like someone she didn't know at all. And yet she had only to meet his eyes to feel something inside her collapse.

"What do you plan to do, Darryn? Go straight back to work at the studio?"

"Yes. If that suits Margo. I'll let her know I'm here." Her voice was shaking and she wished he'd say good-bye and go. She wondered if he'd kiss her and felt weak at the thought.

"Then at least I'll know where you are," he said. "I'll call in and see you before I fly back to Moon Mountain. Until then, good-bye." He pulled her to him briefly and kissed her on the lips, not passionately but as if they'd known each other a long time, as if they were used to one another. It was worse somehow than if he'd been deliberately sensuous, and she felt tears sting her eyes and a lump come to her throat. She turned away quickly the minute he released her.

"You'd better go," she said. "Don't—" On the verge of telling him not to call in before he left, she stopped. She wasn't going to make a point of it. "Don't keep Cyrilla waiting," she said instead. She was repeating herself, and she knew it wasn't Cyrilla he was concerned about. It was Ellen.

He looked at her wryly. "I'll see you later, Darryn."

When he'd gone, she collapsed on the bed shivering.

She didn't go out to lunch and she didn't present herself at the studio. It was after three o'clock when she finally rang Margo to tell her she was back in town.

"Come down and have a talk, Darryn," Margo said instantly. "I'm not busy at the moment."

"I won't come till tomorrow if you don't mind, Margo," Darryn said. "I'm rather tired." That was true enough, but she knew it wasn't her real reason. She didn't want to miss Eyre—though surely one painful good-bye was enough . . .

"Very well, my dear. Did Eyre bring you into town? He flew down for the funeral, I suppose."

"Yes," Darryn said, and there was a little pause.

"Then I'll see you in the morning," Margo said. "It's going to be a fairly busy day so I'll be glad of your help. Have a good rest, and tell me all about your visit to Moon Mountain tomorrow. Thanks for calling, my dear. Good-bye."

Darryn hung up and looked at her watch. The funeral service must have been over long ago, and she wondered nervously what Eyre was doing now, and how long it would be before she could expect him. Possibly he wouldn't come at all. His thoughts would all be for Ellen.

She lay down on the bed and closed her eyes, and after what seemed a long time, she fell asleep.

When she woke it was dark and for a moment she wondered where she was. She switched on the light and looked at her watch. It was nearly eight o'clock, and Eyre hadn't come. Well, what had she expected?

She got up reluctantly and even more reluctantly forced herself to dress and to go out and eat.

She was back in less than an hour, and she sat down and determinedly began to write to her mother and Richard. Anything to stop her from thinking of Eyre.

"Dear Mother and Father," she wrote, and stopped there.

It gave her a strange feeling to write "Father," and she felt a rush of affection for Richard. She was beginning to realise that her mother had been right; Richard was her father. The man she'd met at Moon Mountain could never be that in the full sense of the word. She'd shared most of her life with Richard Ross, and nothing could alter that. If she hadn't formed a very close relationship with him—or her mother—it wasn't because they hadn't been good parents. But as Eyre had guessed, she wasn't essential to their happiness. Had it been to compensate for that that she'd imagined herself closer to Chris? Only to discover that she wasn't essential to his happiness either.

And that he wasn't essential to hers, she reflected somberly. All she wanted in the whole world was one man's love, and that was something she couldn't have.

She had no heart for writing to her parents after all. She wasn't ready to tell them about Moon Mountain or her encounter with her father. She'd have to leave it until she'd settled back into work with Margo.

Which, she realised later as she lay sleepless in bed staring into the darkness, she was not going to do.

She could never be happy living in Alice Springs now. Falling in love with Eyre had put an end to all that. He'd said, "It's a hell of a long way to Alice after sundown," but for Darryn it wasn't going to be nearly far enough. As long as she was here she'd never get over him. Seeing him sometimes, hearing his name mentioned and finally linked openly with Ellen Dwyer's—

She'd go back to Sydney and start again. Her mother would think she'd been right; the glamour of the outback had worn off very quickly.

Next day at the studio, Margo was so busy Darryn didn't have a chance to talk to her until late in the afternoon when they sat having a coffee together.

Margo asked about her stay at Moon Mountain and Darryn answered with pretended cheerfulness, playing up the photographs she'd taken around the homestead and at the muster camp. But quite plainly, Margo was more interested in Harry Dwyer's death, and she soon swung the conversation round to that topic.

"A death is always a shock, but though it may sound callous to say it, Ellen will soon get over it. It wasn't a happy marriage. Of course she should never have married a man so much older than herself and Harry was like a really old man after he had his first stroke. There are happier times ahead of her now, thank God." She dropped her voice. "You were—discreet, Darryn? You didn't hint at knowing anything of what I told you while you were at Moon Mountain?"

Darryn swallowed. "I didn't say a word."

"They'll have to wait a while, of course, but I'm sure—"

Darryn tried not to listen, and the moment Margo stopped speaking, she seized the opportunity to say what was on her mind.

"Margo—there's something I have to tell you. I'm not going to stay on in Alice Springs after all."

"What?" Margo stared at her uncomprehendingly. "But I thought it was all decided. What's happened? Has something upset you?"

Darryn forced a smile. "No, of course not. I want to go back home, that's all."

"Well, I'm really surprised," Margo said. "I thought you were so keen on working here." Her glance suddenly sharpened. "You didn't let Eyre Madison get under your skin some way, did you? I warned you—"

Darryn's cheeks crimsoned. "It's nothing to do with Eyre Madison, Margo," she lied. "I told you—I want to go home."

Margo shook her head and tut-tutted. "Then in that case it's no use trying to persuade you to stay. How soon do you plan to leave?"

"As soon as I can arrange it," Darryn admitted.

"I must say I'm badly disappointed," was Margo's final comment. "However, I suppose no real harm's been done."

Darryn didn't agree. From her point of view, a great deal of harm had been done—to her heart, to her life. Nothing could ever be the same again.

The next day, she made arrangements to take the plane for Sydney the following afternoon. She sent a telegram to her mother to let her know to expect her, then went to the studio where she told Margo her plans and accepted her invitation to have lunch. Over coffee and quiche and salad, she learned that Eyre had flown Ellen home to Linette Downs. Margo had heard the news from a mutual friend who said she believed Eyre was going to buy Ellen out.

"I said nothing," Margo told Darryn. "But of course he won't be buying her out. He'll simply find a manager —someone who'll suit him."

Darryn nodded and tried to tell herself that none of this mattered to her. Determinedly, she began to talk about Sydney.

When Margo returned to work, Darryn idled along Todd Street looking in various shop windows, buying a few souvenirs, and trying desperately to escape from her thoughts, which were all of Eyre. She sat in a cafe and drank iced coffee and began to plan what she'd do in Sydney, but the fact was she simply didn't care. In no time her thoughts were back with Eyre and Moon Mountain—and the darkroom he'd talked of setting up for her there. How lovely it would have been to live there, to—

She got up impatiently and went into the street again.

As she walked back to the motel she heard a plane flying overhead. It was a small plane, like Eyre's. In fact, she almost thought it *was* Eyre's. If it was, he was probably ferrying Ellen Dwyer about. In any case, she didn't want to know about it.

She found that the sight of her lonely motel room depressed her almost to tears. But she wasn't going to sit there crying all night. She'd go out somewhere. Anywhere. Forget him. Or try to . . .

She showered and washed her hair, and caught herself out fantasising as she dressed. She'd chosen the

jade green outfit she'd worn the first time she had
dinner with Eyre and she'd even set out the silvery
green leaves she'd pinned in her hair that night—a
night that seemed to belong in some other lifetime.

She positively wasn't going to indulge in melodrama,
to step out with a memory. She was going to wear
something that didn't have any nostalgic associations
with Eyre Madison. She'd pulled the jade green dress
back over her head and tossed it down on the bed when
the telephone rang.

"Miss Ross? There's someone to see you."

"Who is it?" she asked, and imagined afterwards that
she'd known the answer to her question before it came.
Simply by the crazy way her heart was beating. That
plane—it had been his.

"It's Mr. Madison, Miss Ross."

Her heart beat even more wildly. She knew that if
she had any sense she'd refuse to see him, but she
didn't have any sense. Not any at all where Eyre
Madison was concerned . . .

"Tell him I'll be right out," she said shakily. She
hung up and stood staring ahead of her, one hand at her
breast, the other on her lips. What did he want?

Calm down, she told herself sternly. *There's nothing
to get excited about.*

But she was excited. Her heart was hammering and
she could hardly control the trembling of her fingers as
she took up the green dress again.

It was worse still when she tried to pin up her hair.
Her fingers simply wouldn't obey her commands. What
did he want? she wondered again, staring wide-eyed at
her reflection. What surprise—or shock—was he going
to spring on her this time? Maybe he was going to ask
her to his wedding! But of course he wasn't. Eyre
Madison would never announce his forthcoming marriage only two days after the funeral of the bride-to-be's
husband.

Someone knocked at the door and she hurried across to open it, her hair falling about her face. It was Eyre, not dressed formally as he had been the last time she'd seen him, but wearing tight jeans and a matching jacket, the silver streak in his hair giving him a madly distinguished look, his disconcerting blue eyes seeking hers as she looked up at him stunned.

"You were so long coming I couldn't wait," he said abruptly. He stepped past her into the room, pushed the door shut and leaned against it. His eyes wandered over her slowly, taking in the tumbled loops of her shining hair, the jade green dress that showed off her slender figure, her pointed breasts. Darryn simply stood where she was, staring back at him, her head whirling with a hundred confused thoughts.

"If you're going out with someone, Darryn," he said thickly, "you'd better cancel it. Or did Margo call you up and tell you I was at the studio looking for you?"

"No. What—what do you want?" she quavered. She backed away from him, but he followed her, his eyes never leaving her face.

"I want to know why the hell you're going back to Sydney when you told me quite plainly you'd be working in Alice."

"I—I changed my mind, that's all."

"Why?" He shot the word at her so fiercely it made her blink.

He had no right to question her about her decisions, she told herself, and drew a deep breath. "I've had enough of the outback, Mr. Madison. There's—there's nothing to keep me here. I've done all you asked of me, so I don't see that it concerns you what I decide to do."

"Don't you indeed?" He raised one eyebrow and moved so that he stood only inches from her. "Are you quite sure about that—*Miss Ross?* You really think it's of no concern to me what you do?"

"I—I just don't know what you're talking about."

Darryn's head was beginning to spin and she could feel the rise and fall of her breast as she looked back into his eyes. She suddenly felt so weak she knew that if he were merely to raise his little finger she'd go straight into his arms and beg him to make love to her.

Before that could happen, she turned away quickly to the mirror and reached for her comb.

She dropped it soundlessly as he came to stand behind her and put his arms gently around her, letting his hands rest on her breasts. She should have pulled away but she stood motionless and unresisting, feeling a shiver run through her body.

"Why do you think I came back here after I took Ellen and her sister to Linette Downs, Darryn?" he asked quietly.

"Why?" she whispered. She felt his hands move on her breasts and her eyes met his in the mirror. Something was happening that she hadn't meant to happen. She was weakening, melting, in a moment she'd be helpless. And already she didn't care. The warmth of his hands against the softness of her body was infinitely disturbing and she was suddenly conscious of the bed in the room.

She caught her breath as his lips brushed the side of her cheek and he murmured close to her ear, "Don't you know I think of you day and night? I couldn't get in to see you after the funeral but you haven't been out of my mind for a single minute. You can't go away now, Darryn."

Deeply aware of the effect his nearness was having on her, Darryn pulled away from him. She was mad to listen to him, to take any notice of what he was saying to her, and yet she couldn't help it. She told herself feverishly that he was only here because Ellen's sister was with her at Linette Downs. That meant it would be difficult for her and Eyre to get together. So she was going to use her head—resist his charm—not listen to her heart.

"I've wired my parents to expect me tomorrow," she said weakly. "I—I have to go."

"Then if you feel that way," he said, his eyes burningly intent, "it seems I have no option but to ask you here and now to marry me."

Darryn's lashes flew up and she stared at him incredulously. Her legs seemed to have given way and she sank down on the side of the bed. She must be hearing things. He couldn't have said what she thought he had. Unless—unless he was planning more devious ways of protecting Ellen Dwyer from gossip, she thought ridiculously. *Oh no—Ellen Dwyer hasn't been having an affair with Eyre Madison. He's engaged to that redheaded girl who's working for Margo Talbot. Not exactly a good match—*

She felt the mattress give slightly as Eyre sat down near her and put his arm around her.

"Don't look so stunned, Darryn. You can't be all that surprised when we've been drawn to each other like magnets right from the start. I appreciate that you're reluctant to plunge into marriage with someone you feel you don't know terribly well—and I think I can guess why—but if you're leaving here—or planning to—then I have to rush my fences and tell you that I love you—I want you to marry me. If it's too soon to ask you to make me any promises, darling, at least I hope you'll think about it seriously."

Darryn still stared at him speechlessly. She couldn't believe it. Don't be so cruel, she wanted to say. Don't tease me.

Before she could find her voice, he'd swept her passionately into his arms and he was kissing her the way she wanted to be kissed, pulling her down on the bed with him, his fingers thrusting aside her dress to find the softness of her breast, his body hard and urgent against her own. She still couldn't take it all in, but as his kisses grew deeper and her own responses more intense, she began to believe he really meant what he'd said. He loved her. And oh—it wasn't too soon to ask her to make any promises. She knew exactly how she felt about him. She couldn't live without him. She'd been mad to imagine she could.

"Oh Eyre," she sighed at last. "I'm so happy I can't believe it. Of course I—"

She broke off with a shock and sat up abruptly, pushing her tangled hair back from her face. What on earth was she thinking of? She couldn't possibly marry him. Kate would be dead set against it when she knew who her father was. And even if Eyre was more broad-minded, she had no intention of causing friction in the family.

She stared down at him, lying on his back on the bed watching her, and her mouth trembled. It was going to be terribly hard to tell him, to bring an end to everything before it had even begun.

"Go on, say it," he said softly, unsuspectingly. "Say you love me, Darryn, and then come back here into my arms while I persuade you to marry me."

Tears welled up in her eyes. "It's no use, Eyre. I can't marry you. It would never work. Your family wouldn't like it. Kate's talked to me—I know what she wants for you."

He sat up, swinging his feet to the floor. "Now what on earth is this all about, Darryn? I know exactly what Kate thinks of you. We talked about you today before I flew down to Alice. I told her how I felt about you and she was delighted. So what's bothering you? Come on—out with it."

Darryn's eyes darkened. "It's my father," she said at last, her voice low. "I—I told you when I first went to

Moon Mountain that I wasn't suitable house-guest material for the Madisons. You see—"

She stopped. He was looking at her thoughtfully, his glance moving from her mouth to her eyes and then to her hair.

"I think I already know what you're trying to tell me, Darryn. It's something I intended asking you about later as a matter of fact. You're Chris Beresford's daughter, aren't you?"

Her eyes widened in surprise. "Who—who told you?" she stammered.

"Nobody," he said. "I've been putting two and two together, that's all. But before I go into that I'd like to make it quite plain that Chris—your father—is a man I admire and respect and like. And I can say the same on behalf of Kate. What's more, I suspect my wonderful grandmother had done her sums long before I did mine. It was only today as I was flying here thinking of you and of various things Kate had said that everything began to click into place."

"How do you mean?" she murmured. But before he answered he reached out and pulled her down onto his knee. She went willingly, knowing deep inside her that somehow, miraculously, everything was going to come right.

"I was thinking of the way you'd hung around my head stockman—and of how jealous I'd been. And of that hair of yours that you said was the same colour as your mother's. And of the fact you were so keen to visit Moon Mountain. It wasn't just to take photographs, was it? You knew he was there—"

"I didn't know," she said breathlessly. "I—I only knew that they had been there before I was born—he and my mother."

"Kate told me," he said when she paused. "At least, she told me you reminded her of the little bride Chris brought home when he first worked at Moon Mountain. A girl with hair the colour of a new penny—just like yours—who disappeared inside her bungalow the minute Kate came into sight. Well—the Missus must have been pretty terrifying with her stockwhip and the fierce manner I believe she adopted to go with her heavy responsibilities."

"My mother told me about her," Darryn said with a little laugh, and then she suddenly sobered. "But what about Ellen, Eyre? Margo said—" She stopped abruptly at the look on his face.

"Ellen?" he repeated, frowning. "For heaven's sake, darling, what has Ellen got to do with this conversation?" Darryn said nothing but he persisted. "You'd better tell me, Darryn. Let's not have any more misunderstandings."

She bit her lip. "Margo Talbot said there was— something between you. And I thought you wanted to—to protect her name. That that was really why you'd asked me to Moon Mountain."

"I invited you to Moon Mountain because you fascinated me, if you want to know," he said. "Admittedly you were a help, but I could have coped with the situation on my own. . . . As for Ellen, I've never made love to her even in words, whatever Margo Talbot may have told you. Margo's a charming lady but she's a romanticist and she loves intrigue. She's a friend of Ellen's and I daresay she built up a romantic story around whatever Ellen chose to tell her."

"But you spent all that time at Linette Downs," Darryn faltered, and he raised his eyebrows quizzically and looked down at her, stroking back her hair.

"So you were jealous, were you darling?" he said with a smile. "You needn't have been. Harry needed my help, and for his sake I tolerated Ellen, but she's not the sort of woman I care for. She's something of a man-eater—as Chris could tell you. She's going to sell

Linette Downs, by the way, and Kate and I are talking of buying it. We were discussing whether Chris might consider taking on the job of manager. Do you think you could use your influence?"

"Not really," Darryn said with a grimace. The problems of her relationship with Chris were something she'd talk to Eyre about another time. She hoped her father would take the position and not banish himself to the Barkly Tableland. That way, she'd be able to share some of her future with him and perhaps that wonderful rapport she'd dreamed about would finally flourish. Especially if she and Eyre had children . . .

He'd drawn her into his arms and was kissing her passionately, and when he let her go it was to ask her urgently, "How long must I wait before you marry me, darling? I guess we'll have to telephone your mother and tell her not to expect you home tomorrow. What do you think her reaction will be when we tell her we're going to be married?"

Darryn laughed a little. "She's going to warn me it will be a disaster."

"We'll soon prove otherwise," Eyre murmured, holding her closer and kissing her again.

Darryn knew they would. She closed her eyes and relaxed blissfully in his arms. It seemed she was to find her Dreaming after all.

Silhouette ❦ *Romance*

15-Day Free Trial Offer
6 Silhouette Romances

6 Silhouette Romances, free for 15 days! We'll send you 6 new Silhouette Romances to keep for 15 days, absolutely free! If you decide not to keep them, send them back to us. You pay nothing.

Free Home Delivery. But if you enjoy them as much as we think you will, keep them by paying the invoice enclosed with your free trial shipment. We'll pay all shipping and handling charges. You get the convenience of Home Delivery and we pay the postage and handling charge each month.

Don't miss a copy. The Silhouette Book Club is the way to make sure you'll be able to receive every new romance we publish before they're sold out. There is no minimum number of books to buy and you can cancel at any time.

This offer expires April 30, 1984

Silhouette Book Club, Dept. **SRSR7D**
120 Brighton Road, Clifton, NJ 07012

Please send me 6 Silhouette Romances to keep for 15 days, absolutely free. I understand I am not obligated to join the Silhouette Book Club unless I decide to keep them.

NAME_____

ADDRESS_____

CITY_____STATE_____ZIP_____

Silhouette Romance

IT'S YOUR OWN SPECIAL TIME
*Contemporary romances for today's women.
Each month, six very special love stories will be yours
from SILHOUETTE. Look for them wherever books are sold
or order now from the coupon below.*

$1.50 each

☐ 5 Goforth	☐ 28 Hampson	☐ 54 Beckman	☐ 83 Halston
☐ 6 Stanford	☐ 29 Wildman	☐ 55 LaDame	☐ 84 Vitek
☐ 7 Lewis	☐ 30 Dixon	☐ 56 Trent	☐ 85 John
☐ 8 Beckman	☐ 32 Michaels	☐ 57 John	☐ 86 Adams
☐ 9 Wilson	☐ 33 Vitek	☐ 58 Stanford	☐ 87 Michaels
☐ 10 Caine	☐ 34 John	☐ 59 Vernon	☐ 88 Stanford
☐ 11 Vernon	☐ 35 Stanford	☐ 60 Hill	☐ 89 James
☐ 17 John	☐ 38 Browning	☐ 61 Michaels	☐ 90 Major
☐ 19 Thornton	☐ 39 Sinclair	☐ 62 Halston	☐ 92 McKay
☐ 20 Fulford	☐ 46 Stanford	☐ 63 Brent	☐ 93 Browning
☐ 22 Stephens	☐ 47 Vitek	☐ 71 Ripy	☐ 94 Hampson
☐ 23 Edwards	☐ 48 Wildman	☐ 73 Browning	☐ 95 Wisdom
☐ 24 Healy	☐ 49 Wisdom	☐ 76 Hardy	☐ 96 Beckman
☐ 25 Stanford	☐ 50 Scott	☐ 78 Oliver	☐ 97 Clay
☐ 26 Hastings	☐ 52 Hampson	☐ 81 Roberts	☐ 98 St. George
☐ 27 Hampson	☐ 53 Browning	☐ 82 Dailey	☐ 99 Camp

$1.75 each

☐ 100 Stanford	☐ 114 Michaels	☐ 128 Hampson	☐ 143 Roberts
☐ 101 Hardy	☐ 115 John	☐ 129 Converse	☐ 144 Goforth
☐ 102 Hastings	☐ 116 Lindley	☐ 130 Hardy	☐ 145 Hope
☐ 103 Cork	☐ 117 Scott	☐ 131 Stanford	☐ 146 Michaels
☐ 104 Vitek	☐ 118 Dailey	☐ 132 Wisdom	☐ 147 Hampson
☐ 105 Eden	☐ 119 Hampson	☐ 133 Rowe	☐ 148 Cork
☐ 106 Dailey	☐ 120 Carroll	☐ 134 Charles	☐ 149 Saunders
☐ 107 Bright	☐ 121 Langan	☐ 135 Logan	☐ 150 Major
☐ 108 Hampson	☐ 122 Scofield	☐ 136 Hampson	☐ 151 Hampson
☐ 109 Vernon	☐ 123 Sinclair	☐ 137 Hunter	☐ 152 Halston
☐ 110 Trent	☐ 124 Beckman	☐ 138 Wilson	☐ 153 Dailey
☐ 111 South	☐ 125 Bright	☐ 139 Vitek	☐ 154 Beckman
☐ 112 Stanford	☐ 126 St. George	☐ 140 Erskine	☐ 155 Hampson
☐ 113 Browning	☐ 127 Roberts	☐ 142 Browning	☐ 156 Sawyer

$1.75 each

☐ 157 Vitek	☐ 170 Ripy	☐ 183 Stanley	☐ 196 Hampson
☐ 158 Reynolds	☐ 171 Hill	☐ 184 Hardy	☐ 197 Summers
☐ 159 Tracy	☐ 172 Browning	☐ 185 Hampson	☐ 198 Hunter
☐ 160 Hampson	☐ 173 Camp	☐ 186 Howard	☐ 199 Roberts
☐ 161 Trent	☐ 174 Sinclair	☐ 187 Scott	☐ 200 Lloyd
☐ 162 Ashby	☐ 175 Jarrett	☐ 188 Cork	☐ 201 Starr
☐ 163 Roberts	☐ 176 Vitek	☐ 189 Stephens	☐ 202 Hampson
☐ 164 Browning	☐ 177 Dailey	☐ 190 Hampson	☐ 203 Browning
☐ 165 Young	☐ 178 Hampson	☐ 191 Browning	☐ 204 Carroll
☐ 166 Wisdom	☐ 179 Beckman	☐ 192 John	☐ 205 Maxam
☐ 167 Hunter	☐ 180 Roberts	☐ 193 Trent	☐ 206 Manning
☐ 168 Carr	☐ 181 Terrill	☐ 194 Barry	☐ 207 Windham
☐ 169 Scott	☐ 182 Clay	☐ 195 Dailey	

$1.95 each

☐ 208 Halston	☐ 214 Hampson	☐ 220 Hampson	☐ 226 Hampson
☐ 209 LaDame	☐ 215 Roberts	☐ 221 Browning	☐ 227 Beckman
☐ 210 Eden	☐ 216 Saunders	☐ 222 Carroll	☐ 228 King
☐ 211 Walters	☐ 217 Vitek	☐ 223 Summers	☐ 229 Thornton
☐ 212 Young	☐ 218 Hunter	☐ 224 Langan	☐ 230 Stevens
☐ 213 Dailey	☐ 219 Cork	☐ 225 St. George	☐ 231 Dailey

_#232 SPELL OF THE ISLAND, Hampson   _#238 OUTBACK DREAMING, Cork
_#233 EDGE OF PARADISE, Vernon   _#239 VALLEY OF BROKEN HEARTS, McKay
_#234 NEXT YEAR'S BLONDE, Smith   _#240 SHARED DESTINY, Hunter
_#235 NO EASY CONQUEST, James   _#241 SNOW QUEEN, Wisdom
_#236 LOST IN LOVE, Maxam   _#242 NO GUARANTEES, Brooke
_#237 WINTER PROMISE, Wilson   _#243 THE LANGUAGE OF LOVE, Saunders

SILHOUETTE BOOKS, Department SB/1
1230 Avenue of the Americas
New York, NY 10020

Please send me the books I have checked above. I am enclosing $_____
(please add 50¢ to cover postage and handling. NYS and NYC residents please
add appropriate sales tax). Send check or money order—no cash or C.O.D.'s
please. Allow six weeks for delivery.

NAME _____

ADDRESS _____

CITY _____ STATE/ZIF _____

Silhouette Desire
15-Day Trial Offer

A new romance series
that explores
contemporary relationships
in exciting detail

Six Silhouette Desire romances, free for 15 days!
We'll send you six new Silhouette Desire romances
to look over for 15 days, absolutely free! If you decide
not to keep the books, return them and owe nothing.

Six books a month, free home delivery. If you like
Silhouette Desire romances as much as we think you
will, keep them and return your payment with the
invoice. Then we will send you six new books every
month to preview, just as soon as they are published.
You pay only for the books you decide to keep, and
you never pay postage and handling.